"History buffs will like the cool notion that descendants of important people are still battling it out (George Washington and Benedict Arnold family members pop up), and readers who are puzzle fans may enjoy being a step ahead of the story." —*BCCB*

"In addition to learning bits of American history, readers will be challenged by the codes and riveted by Thomson's account of the kids' episodic, death-defying journey. A fast-paced quest narrative with plenty of action and a gradually developing bond among the three main characters." —*Booklist*

"Nonstop action is punctuated by a series of puzzles that require knowledge of trivia, strength, and creative thinking to solve." —*Kirkus Reviews*

"Readers will enjoy the deductive reasoning involved and the high-stress situations the kids find themselves in as they try to stay one step ahead of the deadly bad guys. This story has the feeling of a computer game that relies on knowledge of American history to advance. . . . Will appeal to history buffs, puzzle fans, and reluctant readers." —*School Library Journal*

BOOKS BY SARAH L. THOMSON

The Eureka Key
The Eagle's Quill

SECRETS
OF THE SEVEN

The EUREKA KEY

SARAH L. THOMSON

BLOOMSBURY
NEW YORK   LONDON   OXFORD   NEW DELHI   SYDNEY

First published in the United States of America in April 2016
by Bloomsbury Children's Books
Paperback edition first published in April 2017
www.bloomsbury.com

Bloomsbury is a registered trademark of Bloomsbury Publishing Plc

For information about permission to reproduce selections from this book, write to
Permissions, Bloomsbury Children's Books, 1385 Broadway, New York, New York 10018
Bloomsbury books may be purchased for business or promotional use. For information on
bulk purchases please contact Macmillan Corporate and Premium Sales Department at
specialmarkets@macmillan.com

The Library of Congress has cataloged the hardcover edition as follows:
Thomson, Sarah L.
Secrets of the seven : the Eureka key / by Sarah L. Thomson.
pages   cm
Summary: Sam (a puzzle master) and Martina (a history whiz) become involved in a dangerous
quest to find seven keys left behind by Benjamin Franklin and a secret society of descendants,
which, when gathered together, unlock a powerful weapon, so the middle schoolers must
solve the puzzles, find the artifacts before the bad guy does, and save the nation.
ISBN 978-1-61963-731-3 (hardcover) • ISBN 978-1-61963-732-0 (e-book)
[1. Puzzles—Fiction. 2. Antiquities—Fiction. 3. Secret societies—Fiction.
4. Franklin, Benjamin, 1706–1790—Fiction.] I. Title. II. Title: Eureka key.
PZ7.T378Sg 2016   [Fic]—dc23   2015012116

ISBN: 978-1-68119-061-7 (paperback)

Book design by Nicole Gastonguay
Typeset by Integra Software Services Pvt. Ltd.
Printed and bound in the U.S.A. by Berryville Graphics Inc., Berryville, Virginia
2 4 6 8 10 9 7 5 3 1

All papers used by Bloomsbury Publishing, Inc., are natural, recyclable products
made from wood grown in well-managed forests. The manufacturing processes
conform to the environmental regulations of the country of origin.

To Adam,
who always believed
in our American dream

SECRETS
OF THE SEVEN

The EUREKA KEY

My Dearest Richard,

I fear this shall be my final letter to you. Many days have passed since I last rose from my bed, and the very act of drawing air into my body becomes more difficult by the hour. Do not mourn me—I have lived a life of greater wealth and prosperity than most men, and I have assisted in the birth of a great nation. What more of this world can I ask?

My only sadness is that I could not acknowledge you as my son; that we are never to embrace as kin in the eyes of history. Even after my death, you will lay blooms upon my grave with the hands of a stranger. For this I am sorry, and will forever be so. I can only hope that you will forgive me, as your mother who raised you has, for keeping her identity and your existence secret from the world.

As you well know—it was only by chance that your twin brother, William, came to live with us, and you remained with your mother. My Deborah was willing to adopt one illegitimate son, but two? Strange, that though you were not the one raised as a Franklin, you are the one I now trust. Your brother's continued loyalty to the British Crown is disappointing, to say the least—but then, he was never a proper vessel for secrets. But you, dear boy—with you, I can leave this earthly realm certain that you'll uphold my wishes and guard the knowledge I have bestowed upon you with your very life. Your true identity as a Franklin may never bear fruit, but I hope that the great service you are doing for your country will act as a feast for your soul. Of all the secrets of this young republic, none are of greater import than the one you hold.

Trust no one but those within the circle. Remember my gift to you, and the gifts of the other fathers of this country. Keep them safe, and with pride.

I will leave you now. I do not fear death—on the contrary, as with a good sleep, I believe I shall arise refreshed in the morning.

Your Loving Father,

Benjamin Franklin

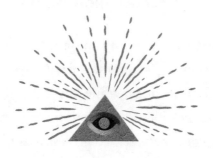

CHAPTER ONE

Sam's eyes were on the clock: 9:54. He sat at his desk, tense as an Olympic sprinter waiting for the starting pistol to go off.

He glanced across the classroom at his best friend. Adam looked even more nervous than Sam felt. He gave Sam a little nod and mouthed *good luck*.

Sam closed his eyes for a moment, trying to calm his breathing and to focus. He envisioned all the students and teachers in the school like chess pieces, set up in their positions at the beginning of a game. And the game was about to begin.

The last number on the digital clock blinked out and reformed: 9:55.

The bell chimed.

Go time.

Sam clicked the timer button on his watch. Exactly five minutes and counting. He jumped up, grabbed his backpack, and headed for the door while the other kids were still collecting their books and chasing down stray pencils.

He zigzagged between the desks and hurdled the trash can.

Fifteen seconds gone, and he was in the hallway.

Ahead was the first serious obstacle—Jason McKay, the lanky eighth-grade hall monitor whose job it was to stand by the bottom of the stairs and make sure no lowly sixth graders escaped from the second floor between classes. Jason was watching the crowds of kids roaming the hallway like a hawk—a pawn who took his job a little too seriously.

Sam reached into his backpack, shoved aside a dog-eared book of sudoku puzzles and his battered Rubik's Cube, and pulled out a thermos. He loosened the top. He had to get the timing just right—it was his first gambit.

He glanced back over his shoulder to see Adam emerge from the classroom behind him and move into position on the other side of the hallway. Sam gave him the nod.

"Hey, Jason!" Adam yelled. Jason turned. "Uh, that red shirt looks great on you. It really brings out the color of your eyes!"

Lame—but it worked. While Jason stared at Adam, wondering what in the world was wrong with him, Sam spilled the lumpy, gooey contents of his thermos onto the floor. Even he had to admit how truly disgusting it looked—and smelled. He'd stirred it up this morning while his mom was in the shower. Oatmeal, raw eggs, vinegar, and cottage cheese. A masterpiece.

Sam cleared his throat, coughed violently, and then groaned. Jason whipped his head around, jumping back as he saw the horrific puddle of yuck on the floor. "My stomach," Sam moaned. "Oh, I think I'm *dying* . . ."

Jason covered his mouth with his hand and waved Sam away. "Gross—get away from me, man! Go to the nurse!"

"Sorry," Sam mumbled, and staggered down the stairs, doubled over as if in pain. Once he was out of Jason's sight, he straightened up and checked his watch.

Forty-five seconds gone. So far, so good.

Sam paused as he reached the first floor, pressing his back against the wall of the stairwell so he could peer out into the hallway. At the other end was the main office, right next to the school entrance.

The seventh-grade classrooms were on this floor, and the crowds had already started to thin as kids made their way to the next period. Sam spotted Mr. Greene, the gym teacher—complete with orange tracksuit, scowl, and a whistle on a lanyard—walking toward the men's bathroom with a crumpled copy of *Uberjock* magazine in his hand.

"One," Sam muttered under his breath. Ms. Lee, the principal, was next. She stepped out of the main office and headed for the teachers' lounge with her empty coffee mug, high heels clacking on the linoleum, just as Sam had known she would.

"Two," he whispered.

A moment later, the front door of the school popped open, and a heavy-set man in a brown uniform backed in with a stack of boxes. "Hi, beautiful!" he called out, and Ms. Ferris, the white-haired secretary in the main office, giggled girlishly.

"Three."

Just like clockwork, Sam thought. But he forced himself to focus again. *Too early to get cocky.*

All the pieces were in place. It was Sam's turn to move.

He stepped out of the stairwell and started walking at a steady pace—not too slow, not too fast—down the hallway.

The delivery guy propped open the entrance door and the door to the office. Whistling, he went back outside for the rest of the packages.

Just before he reached the office, Sam ducked so that the tall counter shielded him from Ms. Ferris's sight. Hunched over, his rubber-soled shoes silent on the freshly waxed floor, Sam scuttled along the length of the counter and right through the principal's open office door.

Two minutes gone.

"What've you got for us today, Jimmy?" Ms. Ferris was asking.

"Oh, just some copy paper, new pens, and ..." He pulled out a single red rose from his back pocket and handed it to the secretary.

Sam glanced back. *Oh, barf.*

Ms. Ferris was smiling at Jimmy; Jimmy was smiling back. There was no one else in their little world—certainly not some kid sneaking into the principal's office. Sam eased the door shut and spun around.

He'd done it.

No mistakes. Not a wasted second.

But there was still more to do.

Sam settled himself into the principal's leather chair in front of her computer. He tapped the mouse, and the computer screen brightened.

A tiny window appeared in the center of the display. ENTER PASSWORD.

Okay. This was it. The moment of truth.

Sam cleared his mind, as he did whenever he had an especially difficult puzzle to solve. *You can do this*, he thought to himself. After all, this wasn't the first time Sam had been in Ms. Lee's office. He'd sat on the other side of this desk often enough. Sure, the things he had done were against the rules—though they should have *thanked* him for the time he reprogrammed the school bell to play the theme music from *Interstellar Zombies*—but they weren't just any old pranks. They were works of art.

Apparently Ms. Lee had no appreciation for art, because he always got detention.

Every time he had gotten in trouble, he'd watched the principal type in her password to access his records. He'd never been able to see the keyboard—but he had *heard* the keystrokes. Seven of them.

A seven-character password. On the face of it, the calculations weren't pretty. With thirty-six letters and numbers, there were over 78 million possibilities. If the password was case sensitive: over 3.5 billion! And if you factored in symbols . . . Sam didn't even want to think about that. But he knew he could figure this out. Sam could figure *anything* out.

Ms. Lee was a no-nonsense type of lady. Sam remembered her typing that password fast—so it was unlikely to be a string of random numbers and letters. No, the password had to be something personal, something familiar.

Sam took a slow breath to steady his fingers and let his gaze drift over the principal's desk. Every puzzle had an answer, and he had a feeling this one was right in front of his nose.

There was a bowl of candy. Two cat figurines—one holding an umbrella, one about to pounce on an eternally startled mouse. A pile of student files. A cat mug with pencils in it. And three photos of the biggest, fluffiest orange cat Sam had ever seen.

Okay, Sam thought. *Ms. Lee is clearly a cat lady. Figures.*

Sam squinted at one of the photos, where he could see a silver heart hanging from the cat's rhinestone-studded collar. It had a name engraved on it. A name with seven characters.

Sam grinned. Bingo.

He typed, "D-I-C-K-E-N-S."

Holding his breath, he clicked OK.

The password box blinked out. The desktop popped up—another picture of Dickens covered with little folders and icons.

He was in!

Three minutes gone.

Sam's fingers flew across the keyboard as he accessed the school's main database where students' records were kept. He typed ROBINSON, ADAM, into a search box. He jiggled the mouse impatiently as the computer slowly processed his request.

A window opened up. Adam's grades.

A whole column of A's, straight down the screen. Every quarter, every class—until the last one. There it was: a big, fat, disastrous D. In gym class, of all things— where you pretty much just had to show up breathing and semiconscious to get a passing grade.

But Mr. Greene hadn't taken kindly to Adam choosing the jazz band over his baseball team back in March. He'd had it out for Adam's GPA ever since. Every time Adam dropped the ball in gym class, every time his shoelace was untied—that was another failing grade.

It wasn't fair.

And Sam wasn't going to let that jerk get away with it.

Two quick keystrokes, and Adam's D became an A.

Take *that*, Mr. Greene.

Sam closed the school records, put the computer back to sleep, and checked his watch. It had taken a little longer than he'd hoped. Four minutes and thirty seconds gone.

Time was running out. All Sam had to do now was get back to class without being caught, and the game would be his.

He cracked the door open and saw Ms. Ferris and Jimmy still chatting it up.

No.

No, no, no—this is not supposed to happen! he thought in a panic. *Jimmy should be gone by now! He was* always *gone by now.*

There was no way he could sneak back out through the office with those two standing right there. He'd be caught for sure. Leave it to Jimmy to sacrifice his delivery schedule for a few extra minutes with his sweetheart.

Sam closed the door again and began to sweat. But there was always an unexpected move to play. He just had to find it in time . . .

Then his eyes fell upon Ms. Lee's open office window.

In five seconds, Sam's sneakers were hitting the grass outside.

Sam raced along the brick wall to the school's entrance. The main door was still propped open. He ducked through and was barreling toward the stairwell when he slammed right into Mr. Greene. Sam looked up at the gym teacher's scowling face, his heart hammering.

"Watch it, you klutz!" Mr. Greene said, and slapped at Sam with his magazine. "What are you doing down here, anyway?"

"Um . . . laps!" Sam puffed, thinking fast. "Gotta keep up my game—am I right, sir?"

Mr. Greene grunted. "Get to class, Solomon, or you'll be doing push-ups in the mud."

Flooded with relief, Sam took the stairs three at a time, vaulted over his own fake-vomit slick, and saw Jason on his way down the hall with the custodian and his mop.

"The nurse says I'm fine," Sam called out. "Just some kind of a flesh-eating virus—no biggie!" Sam skidded around the two of them and threw himself into his seat in Mrs. Ramirez's math class just as the clock flashed 10:00 and the bell rang.

While Mrs. Ramirez was collecting homework, Adam glanced nervously over at Sam from the next row. Sam gave him a thumbs-up.

Sam could see Adam's whole body sag with relief. Sam knew what his best friend's dad was like about grades. Mr. Robinson would have grounded Adam for a month if he had brought home a D. Even a stupid, undeserved D in gym.

Adam dropped his homework on the floor and jumped out of his seat to get it. As he got back up, he smoothly slipped a folded twenty-dollar bill onto Sam's desk.

"Hey, no!" Sam whispered. "This was a favor." Heads started to turn.

"Take it," Adam insisted. Sam covered the bill with his hand as Adam sat down again. "It's the least I can do," Adam murmured. "You saved my butt—big time."

"Eyes up here, please," Mrs. Ramirez called. Math class began.

Sam settled back in his chair with a smile, the twenty-dollar bill curled in his palm.

Checkmate.

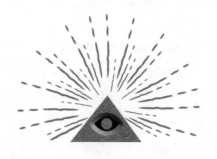

CHAPTER TWO

"I'm home!" Sam called as he walked through the front door to his house.

Sam's mom was perched on a stool at the kitchen counter, and she looked up from her laptop as he walked in. Her nest of curly, nut-brown hair made it look like she had just rolled out of bed, but Sam knew that she'd been working since before the sun rose. Sam had definitely inherited the mass of curly hair—but the work ethic? Not so much. The only thing that could make Sam pull an all-nighter was the Saturday *New York Times* crossword puzzle.

"Oh—hi, sweetheart!" his mom said. "Is school over already? Boy, time flies." She took a sip of her coffee and glanced at the calendar hanging on the wall. "Look at that! Only one more week before vacation. Then the great

Solomon family annual camping adventure will begin! Rising at dawn, swimming in the lake, building fires under the stars . . ."

"Sleeping on the ground, accidentally inhaling bugs, running away from bears . . . ," Sam continued. "Yep, can't wait!"

Mrs. Solomon rolled her eyes. "Very funny, Sam."

Sam flashed her a toothy grin before digging in the refrigerator for a soda.

"Anyway, bugs are excellent protein," his mom said, typing away. "They'll fuel you up for those twenty-mile hikes. How was school?"

"Oh, you know. The usual," Sam lied. "Nothing special." Sam plopped down in a chair, popped the top off his drink, and tossed the paper bag he'd been carrying onto the kitchen table in front of him.

He regretted it the moment it left his hand. His mom was like a bloodhound—she could sniff out a lie from a mile away.

She looked up sharply. Her eyes zeroed in on the bag. Three comic books—one classic *X-Men* and two Japanese manga—had slipped partway out onto the table. Sam could see the gears in his mother's brain turning. He'd gotten into a lot of trouble these past couple months, which equaled no allowance, which equaled *no money to buy comic books*. Her gaze swiveled away from the table and locked onto Sam.

"New comic books, huh?" his mom asked, her tone way too casual.

Man. Why hadn't he gone right upstairs to his room? He was distracted, that's why. Still buzzing from his success.

"Uh-huh," he said, trying to match her tone.

"How nice for you," his mom said. Sam suddenly felt like that mouse about to be eaten by Ms. Lee's cat figurine. "I wonder how you got your hands on those?"

Yep, he was dead. Awesome. Right before summer vacation too.

Sam cleared his throat. "More important, how was your day, Mom?" he asked. One last attempt to change the subject. "I bet it was *really* exciting. You know, out there in the real world. Working hard to provide for our family—"

"Cut the act, Sam. What did you do?"

"Me?"

"Sam . . ."

"Nothing, really—"

"Are you going to tell me, or do I have to wait for a phone call from the principal?"

Sam looked down at the tabletop. "You won't get a call," he said carefully. "And even if I did do something—and I'm not saying I did—it would have been for a good cause. Fighting injustice. Like Batman." He stood, hoping to make a quick exit. Like Batman.

"Don't get up from that table. Sit right there. We need to talk."

Oh, no. Not that. Anything but that.

She rose from the counter and came around to sit at the kitchen table next to him. "Sam," she said. "If you keep this up, you're going to get into real trouble. Not just detention. Not just a slap on the wrist for a funny prank."

Sam sighed, flipping mindlessly through the mail on the table in front of him. He hated it when his mom got all serious. He'd rather she stopped his allowance for another month than look at him with those worried mom eyes.

And what was she so worried about, anyway? He'd pulled off the mission today in five minutes flat. Even though Adam had said it was impossible.

"Look, your teachers have always told me you're one of the smartest kids they've ever taught," his mom went on. "But that's not good enough for you, is it? You think you can get away with anything, like you're invincible. Well, someday it's going to catch up with you."

Sam felt a stab of guilt in his chest, but he pushed it away. Someday, maybe. But not today. And nothing his mom could say was going to ruin that. As he riffled through the pile of junk mail and bills, a glistening metallic edge caught his eye. Sam pulled it out—it was a slender silver envelope, and it had his name on it.

"Are you even listening to me, Sam?"

"Yeah—but look at this! It's for me."

His mom sighed in exasperation. "Fine. Open it. But we haven't finished talking."

Sam flipped the envelope, and as his eyes glanced over the return address his heart nearly jumped out of his chest.

"No way . . . ," he muttered under his breath.

The envelope was from the American Dream Contest.

"What is it?" asked his mom.

"The American Dream," said Sam. "A nationwide contest. But I couldn't have won . . . They must have had, like, thousands of entries."

It had been about three months back that he'd first seen the contest mentioned on several of the puzzle blogs he followed. Then there were ads in magazines. The web was buzzing, especially since the organizers advertised their competition as one of the most difficult, and multifaceted, ever created. It combined classic puzzling—riddles, logic, and sequential reasoning—with American history, and it had been *super* hard. Sam spent almost a week on it—instead of doing his homework, of course—and he'd *aced* it.

Or at least he thought he had. The history stuff—okay, that wasn't Sam's strong suit. But he'd still managed to work out every puzzle and send in his entry.

But that was months ago. When he didn't hear back, Sam figured he must have gotten a date wrong or misspelled

"George Washington" or something. And he shrugged it off. You couldn't win everything.

But now, with the envelope in his hand, Sam's whole body tingled with possibility. What could be inside? He realized it was probably just a note thanking him for entering the contest, or maybe an "honorable runner-up" certificate, but at least it was a welcome distraction from his mom's lecture.

"Well," Sam whispered, "here goes nothing." He tore open the envelope.

Congratulations, Mr. Solomon. You are a winner.

As Sam read on, his heart started pumping somewhere in the upper reaches of his throat. Then a slim paper rectangle fell out onto the table. An airline ticket. "Mom!" Sam yelled, jumping up from the table. "I won! I *won!*"

"What? What did you win?" She grabbed the letter out of his hand and studied it. "They're giving you a trip?" his mom said, dumbfounded. "A cross-country trip?"

"All expenses paid!" Sam whooped. "All summer long!" He leaned over her shoulder to read the words again. "Look at what it says!"

Join me, and the other winners of the American Dream, on this great journey as we follow in the footsteps of our Founding Fathers.

See the seven greatest wonders of our country, from sea to shining sea, from purple mountains to amber waves of grain.

Our first stop will be in Nevada, to tour the desert wonders of Death Valley. Where else will the American Dream journey take you? That we will leave for you to discover. In each destination clues have been hidden to reveal the next astonishing stop on the trip of a lifetime.

I look forward to meeting you in Nevada, Mr. Solomon. Your mind and spirit alike will be altered by the adventures that await you!

Yours truly,

Evangeline Temple

The American Dream Contest

"I don't know, Sam." His mom picked up the ticket, frowning. "A flight to Las Vegas? All by yourself? And it doesn't even *say* what the other stops will be . . ."

"Mom!" Sam begged. "It's educational! It's *patriotic!*" He stared at the skeptical look on his mom's face. She couldn't say no.

Could she?

"You've gotten into so much trouble this year, Sam." His mom sat back down at the table, setting the letter and the plane ticket down in front of her. "It's a lot of responsibility, traveling on your own. What kind of a parent would I be if I let you do this?"

"A *great* parent!" Sam insisted. "The best! The perfect, MVP, gold medal champion!"

His mother sighed. She looked tired, and her hair had frizzed up even more, as if in reaction to her stress. Sam felt that sting of guilt in his chest again. He swallowed and dropped his gaze to the ground. "Look, it says this trip will change me," he said in a low voice. "That's what you want, right?"

"Sam." Her expression softened. "I don't want you to change. But you're better than these silly pranks. Much better."

"When I come back, I *will* be better," Sam said. "More responsible. Different! The letter says so!"

His mom reached out and pulled him against her in a quick, firm embrace. "Not too different, I hope."

"So I can go?"

"I'll see what your father thinks. He'll need some convincing. Go on up to your room," his mom said, and picked up her phone. "I'll call him at work. No eavesdropping!"

"Okay, I promise!" Sam snatched up the letter and the plane ticket and backed out of the room. "I love you, Mom!"

Upstairs, he threw himself on his bed and looked again at the letter. As the sunlight streaming in from his bedroom window hit it, something strange caught his eye.

There was some sort of imprint in the paper itself, and he tipped it farther into the light to see it better. A triangle, with an open eye above it, and a key pointing out of its base. *That's weird*, Sam thought. *What could it mean?*

His eyes drifted back to the last words of the letter. *Mind and spirit alike will be altered by the adventures that await you.*

Sam clutched the plane ticket, afraid it might disappear if he let it go. He'd meant what he'd said to his mom. No more silly pranks at school.

This time the adventure was for real.

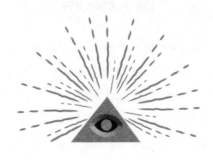

CHAPTER THREE

"Watch out! Coming through!"

Sam barreled through McCarran International Airport in Las Vegas, dodging tourists in obnoxious T-shirts, ducking around grumpy business travelers, catching the flashes of slot machines out of the corner of his eye. His backpack banged against his shoulder blades with every step, the straps digging into his muscles.

Maybe he shouldn't have packed quite so much, but it was too late to worry about that now. He *had* to make the connecting flight! If he missed his plane, what then? His American Dream would be over before it began.

Sam had put too much effort into getting here to miss the plane. His dad had not been too thrilled with the idea. It had taken all of his mom's persuasion, plus a fair bit of begging, bargaining, and promising on Sam's part, to make Mr. Solomon finally say yes.

Sam had solemnly agreed to call often and send post-cards from each stop. It was possible that he'd also sworn to mow the lawn and trim the hedges with nail scissors every single day once he got back home. Desperate times called for desperate measures, and his dad was shrewd enough to realize that Sam would agree to anything just to be allowed to go on this trip.

All that was later, though. For now—he had to get to his gate!

"*Last call for Flight 76 to Death Valley*," a voice blared through the PA system. "*All passengers must proceed to Gate F-4 for final boarding.*"

The flight attendant saw him tearing toward the gate just as she was closing the door. He skidded to a sweaty halt.

"You must be Mr. Solomon," she said.

"That's me!" Sam panted, flashing his most charming smile. He handed her his boarding pass, and she waved him through.

"They're all waiting by the plane," she told him.

Sam thanked her and walked through the door, only to be blasted by a wave of heat that could put a nuclear furnace to shame. It had to be at least a hundred degrees outside. A tiny propeller plane was parked on the tarmac, dwarfed by the hulking 747s all around. Sam almost felt sorry for it.

Three people stood in the shadow of the wing. One of them, a tall woman in a navy-blue pantsuit, watched coldly as Sam jogged toward them. She studied him with dark, piercing eyes, her salt-and-pepper hair pulled back in a tight bun.

"Hey, sorry," Sam gasped as he reached the group. "I ran . . . all the way . . . boy, is it hot out here or what?" The woman frowned and raised an eyebrow. The person at her side turned his mirrored sunglasses on Sam. At first Sam thought he was some sort of bodyguard, but upon closer inspection he could see that this was just a very tall, very well-built boy in jeans and a black T-shirt, perhaps only a year or so older than Sam himself.

This kid was not just big—he looked *serious*. The little that Sam could actually see of his dark-skinned face under his sunglasses seemed to suggest that messing with him would be a bad idea.

Sam tried a smile but got nothing back.

"Mr. Solomon, I presume?" the woman in the pantsuit said, a note in her voice making Sam think she was really hoping he'd say no.

"Uh, yeah, that's me."

The woman gave a slow nod, sizing him up. She held out her hand. "I see. I am Evangeline Temple."

Sam wiped the sweat from his palm on his jeans and shook her hand. It was surprisingly cool, a stark contrast to the blazing heat all around them. "Listen, Ms. Temple, sorry about being late. My plane—"

"Please—call me Evangeline. This is Theodore." She nodded at the tall kid by her side.

"Theodore!" Sam said cheerfully, reaching for the boy's hand. "Kind of like the chipmunk, right?" Theodore reached out his own hand and clasped Sam's tightly. His face didn't change as he gripped, but Sam's did. He tried to smile through the pain as he felt the bones in his hand crunch together.

"Call me Theo," the boy said, not cracking a smile.

Charming, Sam thought, rubbing his sore hand once it was released.

"And finally—Martina Wright." Evangeline turned to indicate a girl standing about four feet away with her face stuck in a book thick enough to be *War and Peace*.

She looked about Sam's age, with black hair chopped off at her chin, the edges so straight you could use them for a ruler. With one finger, she shoved her huge, black-rimmed glasses back up her nose and studied Sam as if he were some sort of rare species of bacteria.

"What's up, Marty?" Sam moved to shake her hand and scanned her black T-shirt at the same time. It had a picture of the periodic table of elements on it. In small letters, it said, I ONLY WEAR THIS SHIRT PERIODICALLY.

"Did you know the first airport was erected on this land in 1942 and was built by a pilot named George

Crockett, who was a descendant of Davy Crockett?" the girl asked.

Is that nerd language for "hello"? Sam wondered. "Uh, no. I didn't."

The girl looked at him a bit disdainfully. Sam could practically hear her thinking that this probably wasn't the only thing he didn't know. "I prefer Martina, if you don't mind," was all she said before she went back to her book.

Great. He'd met three of his fellow travelers, and they included Evangeline the Ice Queen, Sir Theo the Cheerless, and the Geek Squad.

"Time to board, ladies and gentlemen," a man in a pilot's uniform called from the door to the plane.

"Wait, where are all the others?" Sam asked Evangeline as they headed up the steps.

"Others?"

"The rest of the winners?"

"There are no others, Mr. Solomon. You three are the only ones."

Was she kidding?

"I thought there might be more, y'know, adults?" said Sam.

Evangeline raised her eyebrows. "Yes, so did I," she replied. "We had close to six thousand entries, and they were judged by strict standards, I assure you. But it seems that you children were the only ones whose entries passed muster. Quite a feat, I must say."

"Right," said Sam. "Cool."

One old lady and three kids—that was the American Dream? Sam wasn't sure exactly what he had expected. More winners, for sure. Plus maybe tour guides, a photographer, and a reporter or two. It was hard to see how this was going to qualify as the trip of a lifetime.

Since he had Evangeline's attention, Sam took the opportunity to ask her about something that had been bothering him since he first encountered the contest. "So who actually organized the American Dream? You?" he asked. "The ads were a little . . . unclear."

He was being deliberately polite. In truth, the only correspondence addresses had been an e-mail address and a postal box in Washington, DC, that revealed nothing when typed into a Google search.

But Evangeline had already started heading up the steps to the plane and didn't answer. Perhaps she was hard of hearing?

"Don't bother," Martina muttered next to him. "I've already tried asking. I'm surprised you didn't research this prior to accepting the invitation."

Sam hitched his backpack up on his shoulders. "I did!" he said defensively. "But I didn't get very far. Just one dead end after another. What did *you* find out?"

Martina's smug look melted away, and she blushed. "Not much more than you, actually. There's no record of the American Dream Contest registered as a philanthropic organization, or as a company. Whatever it is, it didn't exist before this contest was debuted a few months ago."

"What about her?" said Sam, nodding toward Evangeline, who was being followed by Theo into the plane.

"She's a bit of a mystery too," said Martina. "The public records I got my hands on told me she's the only daughter of Victor Temple, a Boston lawyer, and his French wife, Charlotte. She went to school in France in the 1950s, studied in England, then nothing. Dropped off the map completely for forty-odd years, as far as I could tell, until now." Once Martina was done rattling off these facts from memory, she skewered Sam with a withering look. "Seriously, what have you been doing since you learned you'd won? Packing your sunscreen and playing video games?"

Sam felt the color rising to his cheeks. "This is going to be a long summer," he said, and trudged up the steps onto the plane.

As small as it looked from the outside, the inside of the plane was worse. There were only four real seats, and they were so cramped together that Sam was practically sitting in the cockpit. There was just a little curtain hanging between him and the pilot and copilot. Evangeline and that kid Theo took the two rearmost seats next to each other, leaving the remaining two for Sam and the Wright girl.

Lucky me, he thought.

Sam flopped into a seat and stared out the window. Was that a patch of duct tape on the wing? *Looks like they spared no expense on our travel accommodations*, Sam thought bitterly. But then he wiped the negative thoughts from his mind. He was still going on an adventure of a lifetime, and nothing was going to ruin that. *I'm going to enjoy this vacation if it kills me!*

With a few stops and starts, and what sounded a little like a loud hacking cough, the plane finally got onto the runway and into the air. The towering hotels and sparkling swimming pools of Las Vegas slowly peeled away beneath them, and soon there was desert as far as the eye could see—dusty, dry, and brown.

"This is Captain Hamilton speaking," the pilot announced over a crackly intercom. "We'll be landing at Furnace Creek in Death Valley in less than an hour. Until then, relax and enjoy—"

The rest of his words were swallowed by a burst of static.

Whatever. After that sprint through the airport, Sam was more than ready to sit back and relax. He pulled his backpack up from the floor and pawed through it in search of his phone. Time for a game or two.

"I can't believe you brought all that junk on this trip," said a voice at his elbow.

"Hey!" Sam snatched the pack away from Martina's prying eyes. "It's not junk!"

"Comic books, candy bars—"

"What? Don't they eat on your planet?"

Martina ignored him and went on. "Flashlight—well, I guess that *might* come in handy. And a Rubik's Cube? Seriously?"

"Yeah, seriously. What did *you* bring that's so important?"

Martina pulled up a backpack as large as Sam's own. She unzipped one compartment and showed it to Sam with a look of pride on her face.

Everything was arranged neatly inside, like a jigsaw puzzle of survival. A first-aid kit. Notebooks, pencils, highlighters, and sticky notes. A United States tour guide. Another guidebook on common plants and animals of the Americas. A flashlight—annoyingly better than Sam's. Dried fruits and nuts and protein bars and a couple of bottles of water. And was that fishing line? It was. They were headed for Death Valley, and she'd packed fishing line. She'd probably brought an inflatable boat too.

"You know, I'm pretty sure they have stores in Nevada," Sam said, eyeing the backpack with disbelief. "Did you think we were going to outer Siberia?"

"Well, at least I'm prepared." Martina zipped her backpack with a flourish. "What, exactly, did you think you were going to do with a Rubik's Cube? Kill a coyote with boredom?"

Fine. She'd asked; he'd show her.

"Watch and learn." Sam fished the cube out of his pack. "Mix it up for me."

Martina looked skeptical, but she took the cube and twisted it to jumble the colors. Then she handed it back to him.

Sam studied it, turning it slowly so he could memorize each side.

"What are you expecting it to do? Beam you up?" Martina asked.

Sam ignored the remark. "Have you got a stopwatch?"

Martina lifted her arm to show Sam an expensive digital watch strapped to her wrist. "Of course."

"Time me."

Sam pulled a T-shirt from his bag, tied it around his head to cover his eyes, and tuned out everything in the world except the cube in his hands.

"Okay," Martina said. "Go."

His fingers slid over its slick surface and started to twist. He couldn't see the colors, but he didn't need to. He watched them change in his mind's eye— feeling them gathering, harmonizing. Three reds in a row here. A square of green there. One side was blue all over. Another turned orange.

When it was done, Sam just knew. He pulled away the T-shirt blindfold to admire the solved cube in his hands, and he looked triumphantly at Martina. "How long?"

She looked impressed, despite herself. "Thirty-five seconds." Then she seemed to remember that Sam was a lower life-form. "So that's what you can do. Is that how you won the American Dream Contest? With some parlor trick?"

"Very skilled," said a voice behind them. Evangeline was leaning forward. "You certainly scored highly in the memory and spatial awareness portions of the contest, Mr. Solomon."

Sam grinned.

"Higher, even, than Miss Wright."

Sam grinned wider. He was starting to like the mysterious Evangeline Temple.

"Like I said, it's just a parlor trick," mumbled Martina.

"The whole contest entry was just like one big Rubik's Cube," Sam replied, warming to the theme. "The history stuff threw me a little, but once I got inside the puzzles and figured out how they worked—it was no problem to solve them. Why? How'd *you* win?"

"Knowledge, of course," Martina said, as if it were obvious. "*Facts*." She tapped her temple with one finger. "I have a photographic memory. I remember everything I read. American history is a particular passion of mine, so this contest was right up my alley. I know it forward, backward, and sideways. And since I had all the facts, the puzzle part of it was just child's play."

"A photographic memory, huh? I guess that's handy," Sam said. "Never needed it myself . . ."

"Miss Wright is too modest," said Evangeline. Sam turned and saw she was sitting back, a small smile on her face. "She demonstrates greater analytical skills than many mathematical doctoral students. And she excelled in the linguistic elements of the test."

Sam couldn't help himself. He had to ask, even if he didn't get the answer he wanted. "So . . . who scored highest, me or her?" He sensed Theo rolling his eyes behind his shades in the seat behind him. "And what's your strong point?" Sam asked him. "I don't remember the section about how much you could bench-press."

"Theodore has *other* attributes," said Evangeline.

Sam frowned. Couldn't this guy speak for himself? It was almost as if she was protecting him. Like she knew him, even. Maybe his dad was her boss or something. It wouldn't be the first time a kid won a contest because of preferential treatment.

"And to answer your question," Evangeline continued, "neither of you scored *highest*. In fact, there were several competitors who achieved individual scores above your own."

Sam shared a confused glance with Martina.

"So why are *we* here?" she asked. "Did they turn it down?"

"Oh, no," said Evangeline, lacing her long, elegant fingers together. "You were chosen for your combined attributes. Believe it or not, you complement one another."

Sam snorted.

"She means complement with an *e*," said Martina. "You know that, right?"

"I know what she means," said Sam. He was still bristling from the news that he wasn't the best of the best. Plus, it raised yet another question.

"But why do you need two people to complement each—"

"Water?"

Sam jumped a little. The copilot was standing in front of them with some paper cups of water on a tiny tray. First-class service on this airline, for sure.

Martina passed on the water, but Sam took a cup. The copilot moved on, handing out drinks to Evangeline and Theo before returning to the cockpit.

Sam could have continued badgering Evangeline for answers, but a quick glance revealed both her and Theo lost in their own thoughts. Behind Martina, Evangeline was sipping from her cup and staring out the window. Across the tiny aisle from her, Theo, his sunglasses still on, swallowed his water in one mighty gulp and then crushed the paper cup in his hand as if it had insulted him somehow.

There'll be plenty of time for questions later, Sam thought, *when we're not trapped inside a rattling metal death trap thousands of feet in the air.* He turned back and reached for his water, wishing it were Coke. Martina pulled a bottle of water from her backpack.

"What's wrong with what everyone else is drinking?" Sam asked. "Let me guess: you only drink water hauled by wild goats from the top of Mount Everest or something?"

Martina took a tiny sip of water and cleared her throat. "On a plane like this," she said, "the likelihood that this water is filtered is very small, so it may be contaminated with high levels of mercury, and with the air circulation system there's a good chance that—"

"Ugh, forget it. I'm sorry I asked," Sam mumbled, and lifted the cup to his open mouth.

At that moment, something bumped into his seat from behind, knocking the cup out of Sam's hands. "Hey!" Sam exclaimed, trying to brush the water from his pants before it soaked in. Was Theo *kicking* his seat? Did every kid on this trip have it in for him?

"Dude, what is your problem?" Sam demanded, turning around.

But all he could see was the top of Theo's head. The boy had slumped forward, and his face was pressed against the back of Sam's seat.

"Theo?" Sam yanked his seat belt loose and jumped to his feet. Theo wasn't moving. "Uh, Marty? Maybe you were right about the water ..."

Sam looked over at Evangeline. Her face was pale, and she was looking at him strangely—almost *through* him. Then her eyelids drooped, and she keeled sideways. Her head hit the window.

"I said, don't call me— Oh, my God." Martina got up and stared, open-mouthed, at their unconscious travel companions. She shared one shocked glance with Sam before she hurried to Evangeline's side.

Sam scrambled after her to shake Theo by the shoulder. "Theo! Theo! Wake up, man!" he said. But it was no use. Theo's head lolled back, his mouth slack.

"Help!" Martina shouted to the cockpit. "Please come quick!"

The copilot staggered out of the cockpit a few seconds later. "What? What's ... wrong?" His words were slurred.

"Our friends—something's wrong with them!" Sam told him. He looked at the copilot a little more closely. The man had the same unfocused stare as Evangeline, and he was leaning heavily against the wall of the cabin. "Um, are you all right?" Sam asked.

The copilot mumbled, "I do feel . . . a little strange . . . ," before his knees crumpled and he collapsed at Sam's feet.

Sam stared dumbly at the copilot's body and then at Martina.

"The water . . . ," he said at last.

Both of them staggered as the plane lurched under their feet, tilting forward sharply. Sam managed to stay upright, then glanced toward the cockpit, still blocked by the thin little curtain. The engines screamed.

Please, no!

Sam slid toward the cockpit as if the aisle of the plane had turned into a great big slide, grabbing at anything he could reach to keep his balance. He half fell through the curtain and felt his stomach contract into a cold ball of dread.

Just as he'd feared, the pilot's unconscious form was slumped over the controls. All that Sam could see through the plane's windshield was the ground. And it was getting closer.

Martina stumbled up behind him. "We're going to die," she whispered.

"No!" he shouted. Sam looked back at the prone copilot, and then at the ground rushing toward them. One of the instruments was beeping loudly, and red lights were flashing all over the flight display. "Maybe!" he shouted again.

Martina's expression went from horror to determination. "You know what?" she said, pushing into the cockpit. "I'm not going to let this happen! I'm too smart to die!" She started to unbuckle the pilot from his seat belt. Panting with the effort, Sam helped her drag the heavy man out of his seat. Sam scrambled into his place as Martina clawed her way into the copilot's chair.

"Do you know how to do this?" she asked.

Sam surveyed the dozens of dials, switches, and levers in front of him. Many of the little indicators were spinning wildly as the plane dived. Sam wiped some sweat from his forehead with the back of his hand. "Well," he said finally. "I've done the flight simulator on Xbox a lot . . ."

"A video game? That's it?"

"Stop shouting!"

"How about physics? Aeronautics?"

"Seriously, stop shouting! You're freaking me out!"

"Okay, okay," Martina said. Her voice was still tense but the volume was closer to normal. She studied some of the dials in front of her, trying to stay calm. "We're two thousand feet above the ground and falling, and our airspeed is about one-fifty knots."

Sam took a deep breath. "Okay, I'm going to pull back on the joystick and try to level us out."

"It's called a control wheel," Martina told him.

"Whatever."

He wrapped his hands around the two handles of the *control wheel* and pulled back slowly. The plane's nose lifted sharply.

"Not so fast!" shouted Martina.

Sam pushed the wheel forward just a little, and the plane leveled, its nose pointing straight into the thin clouds ahead.

"We're alive!" A smile pulled at Sam's mouth. He'd done it!

"For now," Martina said. "Put this on!" She popped the pilot's headset over Sam's ears. She was already wearing the copilot's set herself. "Okay, Sam. Just keep it steady!"

Just the thought of keeping it steady made Sam's hands start to shake. The plane tipped forward.

"Steady!" Martina insisted.

Sam swallowed and gripped the controls harder, forcing himself to focus. *Relax.* He told himself. *Don't overcorrect. Don't think about exploding in a fiery ball of death. Just breathe.*

"Radio frequency, radio frequency," Martina was muttering, twiddling with some knobs next to her chair. "Okay, I think I've got something!" She pulled the microphone attached to her headset close to her mouth. "Mayday, mayday!" she said. "Is anyone there? We need help!"

A woman's voice crackled through the headsets into Sam's ears. "This is air traffic control at Furnace Creek. What's your status?"

Sam could have fainted with relief, except that one more unconscious body was exactly what they *didn't* need.

"This is Flight 76 from Las Vegas—we have a problem!" Martina quickly explained their situation.

"I understand," the woman said. "I'll talk you through this." The air traffic controller didn't seem nearly as terrified as Sam thought she should have been. It was as if this happened to her every day. No big deal. Pilots were always keeling over in midair. Kids were always landing planes. "First," the woman said calmly, "don't panic."

"Too late," Sam muttered.

"Sam, will you please concentrate?" Martina snapped.

"I am concentrating! Stop nagging me!"

"If you get me killed I'm going to come back as a ghost and nag you forever!"

"Listen *up*!" the woman shouted, her calm broken. "What are you two, ten years old?"

"Eleven and three-quarters," Martina said haughtily, "thank you very much."

A moment of silence stretched out.

"Oh, Lord," the air traffic control woman muttered. "I knew I should have called in sick today."

"Hey, what's that?" Sam asked, squinting down through the clouds at a long black strip cutting through the barren desert. He described it to the air traffic controller.

"That's the runway," the woman answered. "I have you on my readings here in the control tower. You've got to land that plane. And you've got to do it now."

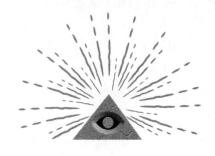

CHAPTER FOUR

Trip of a lifetime, they said! *Mind and spirit alike will be altered!*

Sure, if by "altered" they meant burned to a crisp after a fiery plane crash in the middle of the desert.

"First of all," said the air traffic controller, "you need to reduce air speed."

"How?" Martina sounded eerily calm.

"The throttle. Do you know what that is?"

"Got it!" Martina had her hand on a lever between their seats and was pulling it gently backward. The engine noise died down, and Sam tightened his grip on the control wheel and began to push it forward, away from his body.

Sam's stomach was doing somersaults as the plane dropped swiftly out of the sky.

The woman helped Martina find the controls to lower the flaps and guided Sam in lining the plane up with the runway. All the time the ground got closer and closer. The very hard, entirely unforgiving ground.

Sam risked the quickest glance he could manage at Martina. Her face was pale; her lips a tight line.

"Sam, grab the throttle," she said softly. "I'm going to lower the landing gear."

A moment later, Sam felt a thump through the skin of the airplane as the wheels went down.

"Okay, kids. This is it, you're almost there," said the woman in Sam's ear. "Bring her down as gently as you can."

The blood was hammering in Sam's ears as they approached the runway. They were still going so fast.

"Just hold her at that angle," said the controller. "You're doing well. Ease off the throttle a bit."

Sam's hands wanted to tremble on the control wheel, but he fought to hold them rock steady as Martina pulled the throttle. He held his breath as they dropped down.

The plane bounced wildly as the wheels hit the ground. Martina screamed as she was almost tossed from her seat, and adrenaline raced through Sam's veins, sending his heart into a frantic tap dance against his ribs. The plane righted itself after a few seconds but kept barreling down the runway, straight for a cluster of other planes parked at gates nearby.

"Brakes! Hit the brakes!" the air traffic controller was shouting.

Sam slammed down on the pedals at his feet. The plane slewed and skidded, the wheels screeching. Martina's hand shot out and grabbed his arm.

But finally, the plane slowed and stopped.

Sam blew out a long breath into the silence. "We did it," he whispered. "We landed the plane."

Martina snatched back her hand and sagged in the seat.

"Nicely done," said a shaky voice from the floor. "Kind of rough on the landing. Got to take off a few points for that, but still . . ." Sam twisted around to see the pilot, a sheen of sweat across his head, half sitting but looking like he was about to throw up.

Within moments, two fire engines were shooting down the runway toward them, sirens blaring.

"You can let go of the controls now," said Martina.

Sam looked down at his hands, white-knuckled from his death grip on the control wheel. It took a conscious effort of will to make them release. He heard a sound behind them and spun round to see Evangeline standing in the cockpit just behind them. Her face was still ghost-like, and she was gripping the back of a seat with her free hand, but her eyes were intense as she regarded Sam and Martina.

"Well done, Mr. Solomon, Miss Wright," she said. Then she swayed slightly. "Oh, my . . ." Sam jumped out of the pilot's seat quickly enough to grab her other arm. On his way he stepped on the copilot and heard the guy groan as he regained consciousness.

"What—what happened? Are we on the ground?" the copilot mumbled.

"These two resourceful children have landed the plane and saved us all," Evangeline said, gripping Sam's shoulder for balance.

The copilot managed to sit up, rubbing his face with both hands. "But—but I don't understand. I was feeling just fine, and then—"

"I think there was something wrong with the water," Martina said. "Sam and I were the only ones who didn't drink it."

"But what could possibly have been in the water?" the copilot asked, frowning.

"Diphenhydramine, perhaps," Evangeline said immediately. "Though at that dosage the water should have tasted quite bitter. Gamma-hydroxybutyric acid is another possibility."

Sam stared at her. *Who is this lady?*

Evangeline smoothed her hair back with one hand and adjusted the string of black pearls around her neck as Theo got unsteadily to his feet. "Up you get, Theodore," she said crisply. Theo had a nasty bruise across his forehead, and the big kid looked even more serious than usual. His eyes met Evangeline's, and she nodded at him grimly.

Sam looked back and forth between the two, feeling even more certain that they'd met before today. More important, though—why didn't either of them look more surprised at being the target of an assassination attempt?

Outside, the firefighters were gesticulating wildly.

"I'd quite like to get off the plane now, if that's all right?" said Martina.

The copilot seemed to snap out of his confusion, and he and the pilot went about opening the doors.

His mind spinning with questions, Sam allowed himself to be led off the plane by the firefighters, his backpack clutched in his arms. Evangeline stayed behind, speaking to the pilots as Theo joined them on the tarmac. A paramedic was trying to look at his head, but he insisted he was okay. After the paramedic left to check Martina for injuries, Sam turned to Theo.

"So. Do you want to tell me what's going on?" he asked.

Theo jumped a little, as if he were shocked that someone was actually addressing him. "Who, me?" he said.

"He *can* speak!" Sam crowed.

Theo scowled. "Funny. Anyway, how should I know what's going on? Your guess is as good as mine."

He turned away, but Sam grabbed his shoulder. "Look," he said confidentially. "Someone just tried to kill all of us in that plane. And unlike you and Evangeline, who seem to think this is just another day of near-death-by-explosion, I'd like to know why."

Theo scratched his nose—a surefire clue that someone was about to lie—and looked Sam straight in the face. "I don't know why," he said. "But I'm sure Ms. Temple won't stop until she finds out. I trust her; you should too."

Martina walked over to them from where she had been sitting in the back of an ambulance, and Sam saw her eyes flitting back and forth between him and Theo.

"C'mon, Sam," she said. "We made it. We're okay. Maybe it was just an accident—some kind of contaminant got into the water and no one realized it. It's possible."

"Sure," Sam muttered, unconvinced. "Totally possible." He looked back at the plane, where Evangeline was coming down the steps ahead of the pilots. She squinted along the runway, as if she was looking for someone.

When she reached their side, she spoke softly. "The authorities will be investigating this matter."

"Oh, good," said Sam. "At least someone's taking this seriously."

Evangeline looked at him as if he were a second grader speaking out of turn. "I want you to let me handle this," she said. "You're under the protection of the American Dream Foundation."

"Huh, some protection," Sam mumbled before he could help himself.

Evangeline sighed, and something in her face betrayed a hint of fear. "Listen, Mr. Solomon, Miss Wright. We never anticipated this . . . unfortunate accident. But we will put it behind us. I'll arrange a taxi to take us to the hotel right after I finish giving my statement to the police."

Sam opened his mouth to argue again, but a sudden wave of weariness made him close it again. What was the point? He accepted a bottle of water from a paramedic.

Nothing about this made sense, and one thing in particular niggled at him. Why hadn't Evangeline addressed Theo as well? Just "Mr. Solomon" and "Miss Wright." More fishy behavior. He glanced up at Theo, but all he saw was his own sweaty and confused expression in the mirrored shades.

Soon they were speeding across a barren landscape in a taxi that had probably been white once upon a time but was now a dusty, desert brown. The same color as everything else, as far as the eye could see. Out the window, Sam watched the last of the sunset flaring a sultry, smoky red above the orange mountains on the horizon. Theo had chosen to sit in front, next to the driver, leaving Sam and Martina in the backseat with Evangeline. Martina had her headphones in and her eyes shut. Sam wondered if she was asleep or just avoiding conversation. Anyway, he didn't really care. Sam didn't feel much like talking either.

Evangeline had said they were heading to Furnace Creek Ranch, which would be their base for the trip. She'd even given them an itinerary. Sightseeing, mostly, tomorrow by jeep and the following day with a helicopter ride. After the near-death plane trip, Sam could have done without being airborne for a few days. Other than that, though, the planned trip seemed almost . . . normal. There was another little note about looking for "clues leading to our next destination," so at least that sounded interesting. Sam settled back in his seat, staring at the scenery passing by. Maybe the whole plane fiasco *had* been an accident, and everything else on the trip would go by without a hitch. He was probably being paranoid about nothing; seeing puzzles to solve where there were none.

"Nice," Sam whispered to himself once Furnace Creek Ranch came into view. It was a sprawling, fancy-looking place, the palm trees surrounding it making it seem like a lush oasis of green in the vast empty desert. *Maybe this vacation isn't a total bust after all*, Sam thought, dreaming of late-night room service.

Once they got inside, cheerful people whisked him off to a room so big he could have gotten lost in it. He'd hardly had a minute to sit down on the bed, making the billowy comforter swoosh up around him, before his cell phone rang.

He recognized the ring tone and put the phone to his ear. "Hi, Mom."

"Hi, honey. Where are you?"

"At the hotel. I've been here for roughly six seconds. Do you have a spy drone following me, or what?"

"Ha-ha, Sam. So, is it nice?"

Sam glanced around. About fifteen pillows on the bed, widescreen TV, free Wi-Fi, teeny-tiny fridge with chocolate inside, bathtub big enough to do laps in. "Yeah, pretty nice."

"Good, good. How was the flight?"

"Oh, you know, just a regular flight." In person she would have seen right through the lie, but from a thousand miles away he managed to get away with it. If he told his mom what had really happened on that plane, she'd have him home so fast the soles of his shoes would be smoking.

After promising to call again soon, to wear sunscreen, and not to keep his wallet in his back pocket—*geez*,

Mom—he said his good-byes. Evangeline had told him there'd be dinner downstairs in a few minutes, but even though Sam was hungry, he didn't move. Instead he stood at the window, watching stars begin to appear in a sky the color of the quilt on his bed at home, the same sky he'd almost fallen out of not so long ago.

He hadn't even been on this trip a day, and he'd already had a brush with death. On the other hand, he had also landed a plane, which—though terrifying—was pretty awesome. All in all, it kind of evened out.

What would tomorrow bring? Sam wondered.

⚷

Sam was falling, and as he fell, he was staring at a bank of dials and lights and monitors, all flashing dire warnings at him while alarms shrilled their panic in his ears. But he couldn't understand what the displays were saying, and the ground was rushing up at him, and the alarms kept beeping and beeping and beeping—

With a gasp, Sam wrenched himself awake to find his arms and legs tangled up in the hotel's bedspread. Only a dream. He flopped back on his pillows in relief. But something was still beeping like crazy. He lifted his head to gaze with bleary eyes at the alarm clock on the bedside table. The display read 8:05. He was late! Again!

Sam rolled out of bed and staggered to the bathroom
to throw cold water on his face, shocking the rest of the
nightmare out of his brain. Shirt, jeans, hiking boots,
baseball hat, backpack . . . and he was ready. He burst out of
the room, almost bowling over a maid and her neat stack
of towels. In the lobby, he grabbed a gigantic cinnamon
roll and a banana from the buffet before skidding to a stop
beside Evangeline, Martina, and Theo as they waited just
outside the front door.

"Is this going to become a habit, Mr. Solomon?" Evangeline asked coolly.

"Um, no. Sorry." Sam felt his face getting hot. Martina
was looking up something on her phone. Sam got a peek
at the screen and saw a heading: *Death Valley—Not Just
For Death Anymore!* Theo was too busy doing his statue
impression to take notice of anything.

Sam shuffled along after Evangeline as they approached
a group of tourists who were waiting for the same sightseeing
tour they were taking—a family with two bored-looking
teenagers, a pair of old ladies in red hats, and a man in a
loud Hawaiian shirt and cargo shorts who was already taking pictures of everything with his smartphone. They all
climbed into an open-backed, weather-beaten safari truck
that was parked in front of the ranch and settled into the
seats along the sides. A minute later, the engine rumbled to
life, and they took off in a cloud of dirt.

A man with a sunburned face and an impressively white polo shirt grabbed an intercom and brought it to his lips. "Welcome, travelers, to the amazing Death Valley National Park! My name is Randy, and I'll be your guide through today's tour. Our first stop is the beautiful Golden Canyon. This natural wonder . . ."

Sam tuned Randy out. He'd see the canyon for himself in a few minutes; this desert was dry enough without all those boring facts to listen to. But it turned out he didn't have a choice.

"Did you know that Death Valley is the lowest, hottest, and driest area in the United States?" Martina asked brightly.

"I do now," Sam muttered under his breath.

"Two hundred and eighty feet below sea level," Martina continued. "And the second-hottest temperature in the world was recorded here! One hundred and thirty-four degrees."

Sam tried to ignore her, and instead he concentrated on wolfing down his cinnamon bun and looking at the world around him. Rippling sand dunes stretched out in all directions, and the sky was such a deep electric blue that it almost felt like they were on a different planet. Sam imagined an alien bristling with tentacles crawling over the ridge of a dune as they drove past. Or maybe Theo's head would pop open, and the extraterrestrial life-form animating his body would come out, demanding that Sam take him to his leader. It definitely seemed plausible.

"They also have iguanas, rattlesnakes, and kangaroo rats," Martina was saying, seemingly oblivious to the fact that Sam wasn't listening. "Did you know that the kangaroo rat lives its whole life without drinking a drop of water? Isn't that amazing? And did you know . . ."

Sam began to consider stuffing her NERDGIRL baseball cap down her throat the next time she said "did you know." But then she moved on to something that actually caught his attention. She was talking about the sailing stones.

"Hey! I know about that!" he broke in. "They're huge boulders, and they move across the ground by themselves. It's an unsolved mystery."

"Not anymore." Martina looked delighted to prove him wrong. "Scientists discovered that ice deposits underneath the rocks coupled with the high winds cause the boulders to slide across the land very slowly. Extraordinary, but not a mystery."

"Fine," Sam grumbled. "Go ahead and ruin that too. Ruiner." He nudged Theo on his other side. "That Marty—thinks she's always Wright."

Theo stared at Sam through his sunglasses, stone-faced.

"Get it? Wright? Because her last name is . . ."

Sam could have sworn he saw the edge of Theo's mouth twitch—but maybe he was just imagining things.

At least Martina seemed to get the hint. She went back to looking at her phone and was silent the rest of the trip, until they stopped at the Golden Canyon.

As he jumped off the truck, it was Sam's turn to speak. But all he could say was "wow."

The walls of the Golden Canyon rose above his head in rippling layers. The burning yellow sun made the stone glow as if it had a heart of fire. Sam took a few steps down the path between the curving walls of rock, feeling as if he were walking through a frozen river. A golden, frozen river.

Man, what a great place this would be to skateboard! he thought.

Sam followed the tour group a little ways up the path, barely paying attention as Randy droned on about this landmark and that point of interest. After a while, the canyon walls widened. Smaller canyons branched off on all sides, like a natural labyrinth that spread out for miles. "Feel free to explore on your own," Randy told them. "Just make sure to be back here in forty-five minutes."

"I think I'll take a short rest," Evangeline said, sitting down on a rock. "I'm still a little weak from yesterday's . . . ah, adventure. But you all go on without me. Just be careful—and stay together."

Sam's heart sunk. He had hoped to escape Martina's lecturing for a while and go off on his own.

Besides, he wanted to keep an eye out for clues. The itinerary had reminded Sam that in each destination, they'd find clues about where they were going next. *It's like one of those reality TV shows*, Sam thought, *except I guess the American Dream Foundation is too cheap to bring a camera crew along.* Wouldn't it be great to be the first one on the tour to find a clue? Maybe he'd even be the one to figure out where they were going next. That would show old Always-Wright.

He'd just have to keep an eye out. And if he found anything, he'd keep his mouth shut.

"The walls are mudstone, with some conglomerates," Martina chattered as she followed Sam and Theo along a path that led up a smaller, winding canyon.

Sam tried to keep an eye out for clues, but he didn't really know what he was looking for—something out of the ordinary? This whole desert felt out of the ordinary to him. And Martina's constant chatter was a distraction. Sam could feel his blood pressure start to rise as she went on and on.

"They used to mine for borax around here. They called it 'white gold.' And—"

Sam's patience finally snapped. "And enough already!" he shouted, way louder than he actually meant to.

Martina jumped in surprise. Theo raised his sunglasses and regarded Sam with thoughtful brown eyes. Sam felt his face heat up, and not just from the sun.

"I'll just go on alone, then," Martina mumbled, dropping her gaze to the ground. She stalked past them both and disappeared around a curve in the canyon up ahead.

Theo was still looking at Sam. "She was just trying to be friendly," he said.

Sam harrumphed. "Once again, the Great Theo honors us with his wisdom." He mock-bowed to Theo.

"I only talk when I have something important to say," Theo said, and one corner of his mouth quirked in that same minute smile that Sam had spied before. "Unlike some people."

Sam found himself relaxing a little. "You know what, Theo? You're a weird kid, and I'm a little afraid of you. But you're okay by me." He gave Theo a serious look. "So c'mon, man. Come clean with me. How *did* you end up on this trip? You don't really seem like the puzzling type."

Theo shrugged and looked away as they started to walk again. "American history's kind of a family thing, I guess you could say."

"Your parents are really into history, huh? Are they teachers or something?"

Theo looked at the ground. "A little like that."

It was weird—this trip had Martina, who wouldn't shut up, Theo, who barely had a word to say, and right there in the middle, Sam.

He was starting to feel a little bad for yelling at Martina. Not that she wasn't the Queen of Annoying, but she *had* kind of saved his life yesterday. He'd saved hers too, so it wasn't like he owed her anything exactly, but—

Suddenly, a scream echoed through the canyon.

Sam turned to Theo. "That sounded like—"

Theo broke into a run.

"Marty," Sam finished, and took off to follow.

The two pounded up the narrow path along the canyon. Then Theo stopped short, and Sam nearly plowed into him.

"Don't move," said a quiet, shaky voice.

Sam peered around Theo's massive shoulders to see Martina backed up against a stone wall. At her feet was something that looked like an old coil of dusty rope.

A rattlesnake.

Its head was swaying back and forth, eyes locked on Martina, its forked tongue flicking out to taste the fear in the air.

"I never saw it coming," Martina whispered, wide-eyed. "I was just walking along and it came out of that crack and lunged at me."

The snake hissed and began undulating closer to Martina's leg.

"If it bites me," Martina whispered in panic, "first I'll swell up, then it will start to hurt, then—"

"Stop talking. Don't move," Theo muttered.

Sam bent down and picked up a fist-sized rock from the rubble at his feet. "Get ready," he warned Martina.

"You can't make it angry!" said Theo, putting his hand over the rock.

"Trust me," Sam said.

Theo looked Sam in the eye for a moment before reluctantly withdrawing his hand. Sam pulled his arm back, took aim, and threw the rock at the canyon wall a few yards away from Martina.

Crack!

The snake whipped its head toward the impact. Martina recognized an opportunity when she saw one, and scrambled up the rock face to the top of a huge boulder, well out of the snake's reach.

Theo had the idea now. He tossed another rock, and Sam added a few more, keeping the snake distracted. It hissed in disapproval and uncoiled itself, writhing across the rocky ground before disappearing into a dark crack in the wall.

Sam dropped the last rock in his hand and exhaled in relief. "You okay, Marty?"

She nodded briskly, then slid down the boulder, her hands still shaking. "I bet it has a den under there. We'd better move away from here—we don't want it to come out again." Martina brushed herself off, and with the dust she seemed to brush away her fear as well. "Actually, even if it had bitten me, did you know that only a small percentage of rattlesnake bites prove fatal?" she told them.

"Right." Sam snorted. "That's why you practically levitated up that boulder."

"Quick thinking, Sam," Theo said calmly. "With the rock."

Theo's voice was casual, but Martina blushed. "Um, yeah. It was," she said, looking everywhere except at Sam. "Thanks."

Sam shrugged.

"I usually know what to look out for in the desert, you know, from reading about it," Martina said. "But I got distracted—by that." She pointed up at a patch of stone a few feet above them on the canyon wall. "It looks like some kind of rock carving, but I didn't think there were any petroglyphs around here. I was trying to get a closer look when the snake attacked me."

Sam squinted up at the wall and saw a long, wavy line etched into the face of the cliff. It seemed to be broken into eight pieces. The piece closest to the top of the canyon had a thinner line sticking out of it, like the tongue of a snake. In fact, the whole thing looked a lot like a snake, chopped up into sections. Strange thing to find in the middle of the desert.

A strange thing! Sam thought, brightening. *Maybe it's a clue? Rats. And Marty had been the one to find it!*

"Join or die," Martina murmured, staring up at the image in the stone.

Sam glanced at her. "What?"

"It was the title of a famous cartoon from the time of the American Revolution."

"They had cartoons back then?"

Martina rolled her eyes. Sam should have known better than to ask her. "Not like your comic books, no," she said. "A political cartoon in a newspaper. It showed a snake chopped up into eight pieces, representing the American colonies. And the caption was 'Join or die.' It meant that no state could survive without the others—just like a snake couldn't go on living if it were cut up into pieces. It had to be whole."

"Okay," Sam said. He was surprised—old Marty had actually said something interesting. Why hadn't his history teacher ever talked about snakes? If she had, Sam might actually have paid attention in that class.

"I have no idea what it would be doing here though," she said, shaking her head. "Nevada wasn't even part of the United States at the time of the Revolution."

Ha, that dope, Sam thought, chuckling to himself. *She doesn't even remember that we're supposed to be looking for clues out here.* "So maybe it doesn't have anything to do with the Revolutionary War," Sam hinted. "Maybe it's—"

"A clue!" Martina beamed with realization. "The one about the next place we're going!"

"Ding, ding, ding!" Sam said. "But what does it mean? A clue isn't any good if you don't know what it means."

The two of them studied the carving. Theo gazed at it above their heads. Seconds ticked into minutes, until something caught Sam's attention.

"The tongue!" he said. Martina and Theo both turned to stare at him.

"The tongue?" Martina squinted as she peered closer. "What about it?"

"Snakes have forked tongues, right?" Sam said. "But look—it's *not* a fork. It's an arrow."

Martina's eyes widened. "You're right."

"And there are two letters up there," Sam pointed. "See? An *N* and an *E*, right above the snake's head."

"Yeah, 'New England,'" Martina said. "At least, that's what it stood for in the original cartoon."

Sam thought for a second. Then he asked Martina a stupid question. "Do you have a compass in that backpack of yours?"

"Of course I do. Why?"

"What if N.E. stands for northeast?"

"There's a path to the northeast," Theo said, startling them both. Sam had been so absorbed in the engraving that he'd forgotten about him. "Right here."

Martina and Sam looked at each other. "It really could be a clue," Martina said.

"It's got to be," Sam agreed.

"The first clue."

"You found it," Sam pointed out reluctantly. But he did want to be fair.

"You noticed the arrow and the letters, though," Martina said. Maybe she was actually trying to be fair too.

They turned down the new path with Theo in the lead. "A scavenger hunt in Death Valley!" Sam exclaimed. "Awesome!" This trip was looking up, he thought—or it was until he heard a voice from behind them.

"Hey, kids! Wait a second!"

All of them turned to see the tourist in the Hawaiian shirt coming down the path after them. "You guys down here all by yourselves?" the guy panted once he reached them. He wiped sweat from his forehead with a handkerchief. His pale, doughy face was flushed red with exertion, and his bulgy blue eyes squinted against the sun. The guy looked about as well suited to the rough terrain as a balloon in a nest of porcupines. "Shouldn't go off so far on your own," the guy said. "It could be dangerous, you know."

"We know," Martina said. "But I've got everything we might need in my backpack. I'm an experienced traveler. You can tell the tour guide we'll be back in—"

"What's this about another path?" the man said, ignoring Martina's not-too-subtle attempt to get him to go away. "I heard you talking about that rock carving up there. Sounds fascinating! Lead the way, young lady! I'm sure we'll get some great pictures!" He brandished his smartphone.

Sam and Martina shared a glance. She was exasperated, and he was annoyed—but for the first time since this trip started, it wasn't with each other. This guy was one of those grown-ups who just couldn't take a hint. Shrugging in defeat, Sam said, "Sure, why not?" and followed Theo down the northeast path. Martina came after him, and the man in the Hawaiian shirt brought up the rear, snapping pictures and pointing at things.

Sam wanted to talk more about the rock carving and what kind of a clue it might be, but not with Aloha-Shirt Guy back there listening. He trudged on in silence as the canyon wound through the earth. Now that it was late morning, the sun was beating down on them full force. Sam could feel the heat prickling across his face. After wiping the sweat from his brow, he stared at the mountains ahead of them and stopped dead in his tracks.

"Hey!" Martina complained as she bumped into him from behind. "Why did you stop?"

"Because of that." Sam pointed.

Martina followed Sam's finger with her eyes. "I don't see anything but rocks."

"Do you have some binoculars?"

"Obviously. So do you still think my backpack's full of 'junk' now, hmm?"

"Oh, stuff it and hand me the binoculars," Sam said.

Martina smirked and put a small but heavy pair of binoculars into Sam's hand.

Sam brought the binoculars up to his eyes and focused them. "That's it! It's the next clue! Here, look!"

Martina took the binoculars and surveyed the area. "Let's see . . . rocks, rocks, aaand more rocks."

"Ugh," Sam groaned and took a step toward her. "How could you miss it? It's right—"

Sam stumbled as his foot came down on an uneven edge, and he looked down to see what he had tripped over. He had been standing on a smooth, white stone—almost perfectly circular in shape. *That's weird. It doesn't look natural, so why is it here?* Curious, he looked back up at the rocks in the distance, hopping on the rock, and then off again. On and off. Then he grinned.

Whoever planned this puzzle sure was clever.

"Okay, you have to stand right here to see it. *Here.*" Sam reached back and grabbed Martina's arm, pulling her forward until she stood on the white rock where his feet had just been. "Good. Now turn your head *that* way." He grabbed her on both sides of her head and twisted her face into position.

"Ow! What do you think you're— Oh!"

She'd seen it too. Those three rocks, just visible above the canyon's rim. At first they'd looked like any of the other rocks scattered over the landscape, until Sam's eye had fallen on them as he passed over that white rock.

From that angle, the three rocks seemed to join together, to line up perfectly and look like one long, solid rock. A rock that looked like a writhing snake.

"Another snake," Martina whispered.

"Yeah," Sam agreed. "Just like the first one. Different pieces joining up to make one great big snake. See the head?"

Theo had backtracked and now took a turn standing on the white rock too. He stared through the binoculars for a few moments in silence. Sam thought he saw his eyebrows go up—as if something had actually gotten him excited—but only for a second. "I see it too," he said, his voice level.

"We've got to get over there!" Sam cried. This was a puzzle, and the rock formation was the next clue. A current of electric excitement was pulsing inside him, the kind he always got when all the elements of a puzzle were falling into place. "It's just like the head of the carving. I bet you both twenty bucks that there'll be a tongue—and that tongue will be an arrow. It'll show us where to go next!"

"Wait.Wait!" Martina had his arm."Sam, hold on! That's miles away. We can't just run across the desert like this."

"Why not? It's part of the contest, right? This is what we're supposed to do! And anyway, you've got half a supermarket in that pack, and we've got enough water."

"But I don't have a good map—we could get lost. And how can we be certain these are the clues we were meant to find? It seems so strange that they would expect us to march out in the middle of the desert like this, after the tour guide told us to be back in forty-five minutes. We should at least ask Evangeline if we're on the right track."

"Okay, okay." It was easy to act annoyed, but the truth was, she was right. Sam was getting ahead of himself. The desert could be dangerous—hadn't they already seen that when Martina got up close and personal with that rattler? They needed to be sure. "Fine. We'll go back."

The three of them turned to retrace their steps down the path.

The man in the Hawaiian shirt stood in their way, his mouth pressed into a hard, thin line. His goofy, excited demeanor had dropped off him like a mask, exposing something much more sinister underneath.

It took Sam a few seconds to register that the small black thing in the man's hand wasn't his smartphone. It was a gun.

"Sorry, kids," the man said. "Change of plans. You're coming with me."

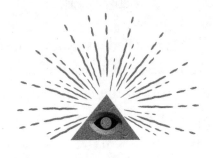

Chapter Five

It must have been more than a hundred degrees out in that desert, but somehow, Sam still felt a chill run down his back. He'd never even *seen* a real gun before—much less had one pointed at him.

"Hey, l-look," he stammered, putting his hands up in front of him. "I get it. You're really serious about vacation photography. If you want a picture on top of that rock, I'm your guy, okay? Just put away the—"

Aloha-Shirt Guy cut him off. "I'm not here to snap pictures. I'm here for you."

Sam swallowed hard, his mind spinning. "But why?" he asked. "We're just kids."

The man chuckled humorlessly. "I know who you are," he said. "I can tell by the company you've been keeping. And I know why you're here in Death Valley."

"For the sightseeing?" Sam suggested hopefully.

"Sam!" Martina whispered. "Shut up!"

"That's right. Enough talking," Aloha agreed. "Now take out your phones and drop 'em."

Sam groped in his pocket, looking around at Martina and Theo as he did. Martina's face was pale under her baseball cap, and her phone slipped from her trembling hands and clattered to the ground. Theo, on the other hand, looked as calm as ever. *Just like after the plane*, Sam thought. *This kid is definitely hiding something.*

Sam tossed his phone down with the others, and a moment later the man's heavy hiking boot came down hard on top of them, one at a time. Sam winced as the sound of shattering glass filled the silence. *There goes my high score on* Hamster Maze . . .

"Good," said Aloha, kicking the phone fragments into a sun-scorched bush. "Now get going. We need to get to those rocks you saw."

Sam turned and looked out across the wide-open desert—miles of dirt and rocks and not much else. He could have shouted for help, but there was no one to hear him.

This was bad.

Really bad.

Swallowing hard, Sam scrambled up a ravine in the canyon wall and then set off with Martina and Theo toward the group of three rocks he had seen just before their vacation turned into the plot of a Bruce Willis movie.

There was no path. Aloha didn't seem to think they needed one. They walked in a straight line toward the three rocks, trudging over baked earth, climbing up little hills, slipping down into gullies choked with dust. Even through his hat, Sam could feel the heat of the sun beating down on him, impossibly hot. If he had been a pizza, he would have been done half an hour ago.

Sam's stomach growled.

Okay, he thought. *Not the best time to think about pizza.*

Theo was striding at the front of the group, his steps almost hypnotically steady. Sam watched him in awe—it had to be seven hundred degrees out here, and except for a few beads of sweat glistening on Theo's face, the kid looked like he was just taking a quick walk in the park. Did anything faze this guy? Maybe he was some kind of government agent posing as a kid. Right now, anything seemed possible.

Behind Theo, Martina seemed to be struggling under the weight of her enormous backpack, which made her look like an unhappy turtle. She kept glancing back over her shoulder to steal a look at Aloha. As if she were checking to make sure he wasn't just a mirage.

Sam knew how she felt. Any moment now, he was expecting to wake up in a camping tent in the woods, his mom and dad right outside.

Sam pinched himself.

No such luck.

Sam caught up to Martina and walked next to her. "I don't get it," he muttered, low enough so Aloha wouldn't hear. "What could this guy possibly want with us? And why does he care so much about these clues for the contest?"

Martina rolled her eyes. "Think, genius," she mumbled back. "Have you considered that maybe those clues *aren't* part of the contest? That maybe we stumbled onto something . . . else?"

Sam furrowed his brows in thought. The clues *had* been more complex than he'd imagined—he thought they'd just find a flyer nailed to a rock or something. The snake engraving, the rock formation—it did seem like a lot of work for one silly contest. But if it wasn't put there for them to find, what were these clues leading to? Sam's desire to solve that mystery was strong, but his desire to survive was stronger.

They had to get away from this guy. And fast—before they ventured so far into the desert that they'd have no idea how to get back.

Okay. Think, Sam, think.

The tour guide had said that the group was supposed to gather again in forty-five minutes. How long had it been? Twenty minutes? More? Soon somebody was going to notice that they were gone. Evangeline would be looking for them.

But it would still take them a long time to organize a search party and to figure out which way they went. Sam glanced back, and Aloha met his gaze with a menacing, narrow-eyed look. But that quick glance had told Sam what he needed to know—they weren't leaving any visible footprints.

This is a Hansel and Gretel situation, he thought—they needed to leave breadcrumbs.

Sam casually stripped his baseball cap off his head and mopped at his sweaty face. And then he let the hand holding the hat dangle for a moment by his side.

Without stopping, he dropped the cap.

A second later, the loudest sound he'd ever heard nearly split his eardrums open. He yelped, and Martina jumped about a foot. Theo whirled around, his hands balled into fists.

Aloha was standing behind them with his gun pointed at Sam's hat, which lay on the ground with a smoking hole through the brim.

"Pick it up," Aloha growled. "The next shot won't be a warning one."

Sam's shoulders slumped. He stepped back a few paces to pick up his hat, fingering the hole's frayed edges.

"Now, let's keep going," Aloha said.

They kept going.

Sam pulled the hat back onto his head. Aloha was watching them too carefully for Sam to drop anything else. And making a run for it was out of the question. Just like he did in chess, Sam went through every possible move they could make, but there were no good options.

In this game, he was nothing more than a pawn.

The ground got a little rougher. Scrawny plants snagged the cuffs of Sam's jeans, and clumps of thorny bushes crackled under his sneakers. Martina gasped as a black scorpion skittered across her path before disappearing into a deep crack in the earth.

After a while—Sam wasn't sure how long—they reached the base of a hill. On top were the three twisted rocks they had been heading for.

Sam stopped to catch his breath, hands on his knees. *Man, and I thought gym class was bad,* he thought.

"Up," Aloha ordered.

Glumly, he started to climb.

Sam hadn't thought that this little hike could get any worse, but it did. The slope was steep, and soon Sam was gasping for air, his shirt plastered to his chest with sweat. Even Theo seemed to be slowing down, and next to him, Martina stumbled and almost slid back down the hill more than once.

Behind him, Sam heard the slosh of liquid, and he glanced back to see Aloha guzzling from a huge black canteen, rivulets of water spilling down the sides of his mouth and onto his Hawaiian shirt. Sam stared at him and made a promise then and there that he would never buy a Hawaiian shirt as long as he lived. Never.

Martina stopped. "We need some water too," she said, turning back to face Aloha. Her chin was up, and Sam was impressed by how steadily she spoke. Aloha didn't say yes, but he didn't say no either. He just stood there, holding his canteen and waiting as Martina dug a water bottle out of her backpack.

She handed it to Sam. He tipped his head back, ready to swallow half the contents.

"We might need it more later," Theo warned. Sam hesitated, the bottle inches from his lips. What if they did get a chance to run? What if Aloha got what he wanted—whatever that was—and decided to leave them here in the desert? He imagined himself wandering for miles, sunburned and parched with thirst. Licking his lips, he handed the water bottle back to Martina, still full.

She looked at it longingly but put it away. They started climbing again.

At last they stumbled, panting and sweating, over a lip of stone onto a flattened area the size of a large patio. A lizard as long as Sam's forearm skittered up the rock face as they arrived. On the far edge of the flat area, a rock wall rose up, the three writhing snake-stones on its top. And below the snake-stones—

"A door?" Martina croaked. "Is that a door?"

Three dark cracks in the dusty stone joined to make a rectangle. *No way that shape is natural*, Sam thought. *Someone put it there.*

Now Sam was certain—there was no way this was the work of the American Dream Contest. This was something much bigger than that, and from the looks of it, much older.

"Hey, Marty," he wheezed. "I don't suppose *this* is in your guidebook, is it?"

Martina's eyes were wide as she stared at the mysterious door in the middle of the wilderness. "No," she said, not taking her eyes from it. "I don't think it is."

"You three, move away," Aloha ordered, pointing with his gun. Without taking his eyes off them, Aloha laid one hand on the door and pushed. He leaned his shoulder against the rock and shoved. Nothing moved. If that thing really was a door, it was sealed tight.

From high up on the hill, Sam could see for miles around. With Aloha distracted with the door, Sam scanned the landscape, searching for any sign of a rescue party. But there was nothing to see but some vultures wheeling through the air above them and the curious black lizard studying them from a rock a few feet away.

The lizard seemed to decide that the four of them were not much of a threat. It made its way to the ground and strolled right by Sam's feet, its tail creating a curving trail through the dust. Sam watched the lizard walk to the edge of the hill and drop out of sight.

Sam looked back at the ground at his feet. The lizard's tail had brushed some of the dirt aside, exposing the ground underneath. Something odd caught his eye, and Sam crouched down and began to brush away the rest of the dirt. When he saw what was there, he froze.

Suddenly, Aloha was at Sam's side. "What is it? What did you find?"

Sam straightened up, startled. "Uh, I'm not sure . . ."

At their feet, carved directly into the rock floor, was unmistakably the letter *M*.

"Clear the rest of that dirt away!" Aloha said. "All of you!"

On their hands and knees, Sam, Martina, and Theo did as they were told, brushing aside the pale dust of the desert. It rose in clouds before settling back over them, coating their clothes and sticking to their sweaty skin. Slowly, a shape emerged under their hands: a huge circle notched with small holes and letters of the alphabet at regular intervals all around it.

"Well? What is it?" Aloha barked. "How does it work?"

"How should we know?" Sam spluttered. "It's a clock, okay? A big, weird clock with no hands in the middle of the desert. Happy now?"

"No, I'm not." Aloha scowled. "I want that door open, *now*. I'll ask you again: *how does it work?*"

"I told you, I don't know!" Sam shouted, his frustration making him momentarily forget about the gun. Why did the guy seem to think that Sam and the others would know what was going on here?

Aloha sighed and rubbed his chin. "Fine. You said it's a clock without hands, right? So find the hands. Search this whole place. And don't try anything funny."

They were all searching for five minutes before Sam heard Martina shout, "I found something!"

Sam whipped around to look at her. She was kneeling down near the stone door. "What is it?" he said.

"I think I know what fits in those holes!" Martina sounded strangely happy, as if she'd forgotten they were in danger and was just excited to learn something new.

Sam made his way over to where Martina was brushing dirt away from something long and thin lying near the wall. With the dust all over it, it just looked like another chunk of rock. But in the trails left by Martina's fingers, Sam could see the ghostly reflection of his own face, his eyes wide with surprise.

It was a huge sculpted object—five feet tall and shaped like a bird's wing—and it was made entirely of glass. Sam and Theo gathered around it, helping Martina to brush it clean. It was a crazy thing to find up on a mountain in the desert. Of course, this whole situation was crazy. *Maybe I've gotten sunstroke and am delirious*, Sam thought as he helped brush off the last of the dirt. *Maybe I'm hallucinating.*

"It's a gnomon," Martina said.

Martina must have sunstroke too. Now she's talking nonsense.

"Part of a sundial," she added, as if she'd noticed Sam's blank look. "The part that casts a shadow."

Okay, not babbling. Just showing off.

"So that clock thing over there . . ." Sam looked at the circle on the ground. "It's a sundial?"

Martina nodded. "I think so."

"Now, that's more like it," Aloha said, sounding pleased. "Get that Norman—"

"Gnomon," Martina corrected him.

"Whatever," Aloha said. "Get it over where it belongs." Reaching into his shirt pocket, he pulled out a cell phone and put it to his ear. "Yes, sir," he said after a moment. "I found the entrance. They're in my custody."

Sam felt his knees turn to water. They weren't just dealing with one crazy tourist—they were dealing with a crazy tourist with a boss. What in the world had he gotten himself into?

Aloha stuffed the phone back into his pocket. "Hurry up," he said. "The sooner you kids put that thing together, the sooner we can get that door open."

"Well, if you helped a little," Sam muttered under his breath as he slipped his hands under the wing, ready to lift it off the ground.

"You're just *trying* to get us killed, aren't you?" Martina whispered, crouching down next to him.

Sam, Theo, and Martina heaved the glass wing up and staggered toward the sundial. The wing had a long spindle on one end that was obviously meant to go into a hole and keep the heavy thing upright—if they could get over there without dropping it.

And which hole was it supposed to go into?

After a few moments of shuffling and indecision, Theo grunted, "Put it down!"

Without Theo's help, the wing wasn't going much of anywhere anyway. They eased it to the ground, leaning it against a handy chunk of rock so that it would not be so difficult to pick up the next time.

Martina flopped down too. "How about some of that water now?" she asked, pulling off her hat to rub sweat and dust from her face. Theo nodded.

After swallowing a few mouthfuls of warm water, Sam stood beside the glass wing. He ran a finger along the smooth, curved surface.

"How's this thing going to work, anyway?" he asked. "I mean, it's made out of glass. What kind of a shadow is it going to cast?"

Martina finished a long swallow and shook her head, handing the bottle to Theo. "I don't know." She frowned. "And what about the door?"

Sam squinted at it. "You think putting the sundial together will really make it open?"

Martina shrugged. "They must be connected. Why else would someone put this here?" A faint wind blew Martina's hair around her face, and blew new dust across the face of the sundial. Seconds later, Sam heard a faint noise—*whappity, whappity, whappity*—that got louder with every passing second.

Sam's head snapped around, and he spotted something heading right for them—a helicopter!

Sam's heart soared. Park rangers! Police! A search party! They had to wave, yell, distract Aloha somehow, and get the attention of the people in that chopper. This was their chance!

The helicopter was closer now, black against the bright-blue sky, its blades beating the air and whipping up a fierce wind that tugged at Sam's shirt and flipped Theo's hat off his head.

Sam was about to raise his arms over his head and shout, but Aloha beat him to it. "Over here!" their captor shouted, waving his arms at the helicopter.

The words died on Sam's lips.

Whoever was in that helicopter wasn't coming to their rescue.

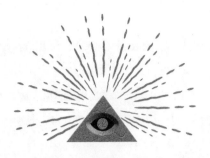

CHAPTER SIX

The helicopter, kicking up massive clouds of red-brown dust, landed on a flat stretch of rock below the plateau where Sam, Theo, and Martina stood. The chopper's blades slowed, and then, out of the dust, several figures emerged.

The first was the tallest, and he stood still for a few moments, looking up toward the three children and their captor. Despite the heat, he was wearing a pristine black suit jacket, vest, and tie over a white shirt. Sam didn't like the way it felt to have the man's eyes on him. For some reason, he reminded Sam of the rattlesnake, the way it had eyed Martina's leg, deciding where to sink its fangs.

There were four other men with him, dressed in hiking gear and heavy boots, carrying packs full of who knows what. At a signal from the first man, they all began to move up the hillside. It wasn't long before they had all arrived on the little plateau. It was starting to feel kind of crowded up there.

Aloha nodded at the man who had gotten out of the helicopter first. "Mr. Flintlock," he said, sounding proud of himself. "There's the entrance, sir; you can see it for yourself. This sundial is the key to getting it open."

Up close, Flintlock reminded Sam of the mountainous terrain that surrounded them—big and dangerous. Even his craggy, sunbaked skin looked like it was carved out of stone. *So here is the master of the game*, Sam thought.

Sam watched Flintlock frown at the sundial and move slowly around it, his eyes unreadable behind sunglasses, his dark hair coated with a thin layer of brown dust. His lips were pressed tightly together in thought as he took in every detail of the engraving at his feet and the glass wing that leaned nearby. It was a look of intense concentration that Sam recognized.

Maybe Mr. Flintlock knew about puzzles too.

And puzzles usually had some kind of a prize at the end. A payoff. Something to make figuring them out worthwhile. *What could possibly be behind that closed door,* Sam wondered, *that made all* this *worthwhile?*

"It's a sundial, all right," Flintlock muttered. "But it needs something to cast a shadow so it can function."

"It's called a gnomon—" Martina started.

Sam and Theo both glared at her. She gulped and fell silent.

Mr. Flintlock slipped off his sunglasses and turned to the kids, as if he had just noticed them standing there. His dark eyes scanned each of them before he shook his head and scoffed. "Kids," he muttered. "They're just a bunch of kids."

"*These* kids can do it," Aloha assured him. "I saw them figure out the clues with my own eyes. Trust me, boss— they're little geniuses, all of them!"

Geniuses? Teachers, principals, and parents had called Sam Solomon a lot of things, but "genius" had never been one of them.

Flintlock looked skeptical. He didn't believe in that "genius" description any more than Sam did. And yet, Sam got the feeling that if he, Martina, and Theo couldn't solve this puzzle, Mr. Flintlock would be very disappointed.

And Sam didn't particularly want to find out what he was like when he was disappointed.

"Fine," Flintlock finally said. "Let's see what they can do." His tone suggested that he didn't expect it to be much.

"Okay, kids," Aloha said, waving the gun. "Get started."

"Hold on a second," Sam said, swallowing his nervousness. "Mister, um—Flintlock? You obviously were expecting someone else, so if you could just let us go, we'd be happy to help you find . . ."

Sam trailed off as Flintlock turned, and he saw the cold expression on the man's stony face. It made Sam think of the rattlesnake again. It was the look of a man not used to being refused.

"Sam." Theo, standing close by, spoke just loudly enough for Sam to hear him. "Better do what he says."

"Good advice." Aloha sneered, his mouth stretched into an ugly smile. Behind him, one of the other men settled down on a rock and slipped a jackknife from his pocket. He flipped it open, using the tip of the blade to pick at something in his teeth.

Sam's heart sunk. Between the gun, the knife, and the human mountain in the spotless suit, they had exactly zero chance of getting away. Not yet. Theo was right—and more than that, a not-so-small part of Sam wanted to see what was behind that door too.

Sam walked over to the sundial, where Martina had already dropped to her knees to study some of the markings in the stone more closely. Sam followed her example, and Theo moved slowly around the circle.

"This is weird," Martina murmured. "Normally, sundials use Roman numerals. I see an I over here for one o'clock, and a V over there for five—but these other letters don't make any sense." She pulled off her glasses to rub dust from the lenses.

Sam scanned the rest of the letters. "Here's a C—wait, no—there's three of them. C is a Roman numeral. And so is this D, and the M."

"True," Martina admitted, putting her glasses back on her nose. "But who ever heard of a clock with a hundred hours? Or five hundred? Or a thousand?" She craned her head and pointed at one of the letters. "Anyway, there's a *P*. Don't tell me that's a numeral too."

Theo squinted down at the ground, listing each of the letters out loud. "*P, I, V, H, Y, J, G, D,* two *M*'s, and three *C*'s. Each one with a hole next to it." He shook his head. "It seems completely random."

"Maybe we're supposed to play Scrabble," Sam said.

Martina rolled her eyes. "C'mon, Sam. Anyway, there aren't nearly enough vowels." Suddenly Sam saw her eyes focus on something just over his shoulder. "Hey . . . what is *that?*" She moved past him and dropped into a crouch a few feet away. Sam hurried over and watched her brush dirt and gravel away from a metal plaque on the ground, inscribed with four lines of delicate text. "I saw a corner of it peeking out," Martina murmured. "We must have uncovered it when we were digging out the gnomon."

Sam peered over her shoulder, and they read it together.

THOUGH YOUR CONSTITUTION MAY BE HALE,
YOUR QUEST SHALL BUILD A MIGHTY THIRST.
IF YOU WISH TO ENTER MY OASIS,
YOU MUST FIRST LOOK TO THE FIRST.

"An oasis," Sam muttered. "That sounds good about now."

"Look to the first," Martina said thoughtfully. She sounded calm, as if she'd totally forgotten the scary guys with guns and knives and mysterious motives, as if the puzzle had taken up all her brainpower and left her no room for fear. "What if we put the glass wing into the hole near the *I*?" she suggested. "That's a Roman numeral one. Maybe that's the first?"

"Isn't midnight really the first hour of the day?" Sam asked.

"Hmm, yes," Martina answered. "But there isn't a twelve. That would be *X* plus two *I*'s, and there's nothing like that."

"It can't be that easy." Sam was starting to feel just a bit better. Arguing with Martina was comforting somehow. He looked at the letters again, automatically counting them up in his head. "Wait a second," he said when he'd finished. "What if the answer has nothing to do with time at all? There are *thirteen letters*. What kind of a clock has thirteen positions?"

"Enough!" Both Sam and Martina jumped at the sound of Aloha's voice, jarring them back to reality. "Enough of this yammering, you two. Get on with it." His gun moved threateningly back and forth between them.

To their surprise, Flintlock slapped the gun down.

"They *are* getting on with it," Flintlock barked. "Back off. Arguing is how these two think." Aloha wilted under the glare of his boss and scurried back to where the other men were waiting.

"Go on," Flintlock told them. "Argue some more."

Sam swallowed hard. "Okay . . . ," he said, looking at Martina helplessly. Being *told* to argue by an adult somehow took all the fun out of it. "So, if the letters are just letters, not Roman numerals, what do they mean?"

"I don't know," Martina said, chewing on her thumbnail.

"I mean, there's no word in the English language that uses all those letters, so they each must represent something else. But what?"

Suddenly Martina shrieked.

Sam almost leaped out of his own hiking boots. "What? What? Is it another snake?" he cried.

"What? No, no, no!" Martina said, waving off Sam's panic like a fly. Theo was watching them both with interest. "What you said, Sam—about the letters representing something. That's it! That's the answer!"

"It is?"

"Remember that cartoon? The one with the cut-up snake? It had letters on it too. Representing each of the original American colonies. *Thirteen* colonies! Let's see if I'm right. Look for the letters. *D* for Delaware . . ."

Theo moved back a few paces as Sam scrambled across the dusty rock on hands and knees to find the letter near one of the holes. "Yep, here!"

"*P* for Pennsylvania. *C* for Connecticut," Martina went on, ticking each one off on her fingers.

"Got 'em!"

As Martina called out each letter, Sam found them. *M* for Maryland and another for Massachusetts, *V* for Virginia, *G* for Georgia. But then they ran into trouble.

"New York!" Martina called out.

"*N, N, N* . . ." Sam went all the way around the circle. "No *N*."

"What?" Martina's face fell. "Then I can't be right . . ."

"And what about these? *Y. I.*" Sam looked up. "No American colony started with *I*, right?"

"No." Martina looked crestfallen. "I was so sure . . ."

Sam looked down at the sundial. He had been certain Martina was right too. He'd had that feeling, the one he got when a puzzle was finally coming together.

Then Sam felt a grin stretching his dry lips as he looked down at the hole in the rock with the *I* next to it. Puzzles weren't always about knowing all the facts, whatever Martina might think. Sometimes what you really had to do was just look at things a little differently.

"Not so fast, Marty. You're right. You're a genius after all!"

"Don't call me Mar— Wait, I am?"

"*I* for *Island*! Rhode Island! *Y* for *York*. They only used one letter to represent each colony—even ones with two words."

Sam saw Theo staring at him with what almost looked like admiration. "Brilliant," Theo murmured, shaking his head.

Despite everything, Sam grinned. "Okay," he said, turning back to Martina. "What's left?"

Martina's eyes sparkled with excitement. "New Jersey, New Hampshire," she said.

"Yep, we have a *J*! And here's an *H*!"

"And North and South Carolina!" she said.

"Those are the two *C*'s left over—that's all of them!"

"So," Flintlock cut in. "Where does that leave us, children?"

Whoops. Once again, Sam had gotten so excited about the puzzle, he'd kind of forgotten the bad guys. "I don't know. Yet. We're getting there."

"Good. Now get there faster," Flintlock said.

"A minute ago you said to let them argue," Theo muttered. "And now you're telling them to hurry up? You should make up your mind."

Flintlock turned his cold gaze on Theo. "Is that so?" he said, his voice like a hiss. "And how about you, tall, dark, and useless? I don't see you doing a thing. Perhaps you're expendable."

"So!" Martina piped up, her voice quavering a little with nerves. Maybe she was trying to distract Flintlock before his staring contest with Theo turned into something worse. "Letters. Colonies. This is the right track."

"Definitely!" Sam tried to back up Martina. If Aloha or Flintlock decided that Theo wasn't being any help here . . . well, that might not be good for Theo. "But how can we be sure which is which?" he went on nervously. "I mean, is this *M* Massachusetts or Maryland?"

"I don't think it matters. The poem says, 'Look to the first.'"

"The first? First colony?"

"Virginia!" Martina crowed. "That was the first colony to be founded. We have to put the gnomon in the hole that's under the *V*!" Martina announced.

"Do it," Flintlock ordered. If he was excited, he wasn't showing it in his expression. He looked single-minded. Ruthless.

The glass wing needed all three of them to lift it. Theo and Sam took the lower half, bracing with their legs, while Martina lifted from the top to keep it balanced. "Just don't drop it," Sam grunted, imagining bits of glass scattered all over the mountainside. Flintlock would probably go nuclear if that happened.

Plus, Sam would never find out if they'd solved the puzzle.

They shuffled toward the *V*-hole. As the spindle edged nearer, even Theo, Sam noticed, had started to sweat. "Careful. Careful, guys . . ." Martina gasped.

"I *am* being careful," Sam grumbled.

Aloha grunted impatiently and moved over to stand in front of the sealed door.

"Just a little more," Martina said. "To the right a bit."

"I know that," said Sam. "I do have eyes. You don't have to keep telling—"

The glass spindle slid into the hole.

The light around them seemed to flare, and Sam stumbled back, blinking madly.

"What the—?" said Flintlock.

Then a scream filled the air. It came from Aloha.

Sam managed to see through watering eyes. A bright beam of concentrated light, like a laser, shot from the glass wing and toward the doorway where Aloha stood.

Sam had never been one of those sadistic kids who fried ants with a magnifying glass. But he knew it could be done. The lens took sunlight and focused it into a beam so strong it could start a fire. The glass wing had done the same thing, only the glass wing was way bigger than a magnifying glass.

Just like a grown man was way bigger than an ant.

The orange flowers on Aloha's shirt burst into red flames. He howled in pain, staggering across the plateau, as the fire took hold.

Sam stood frozen, shocked. Flintlock quickly stepped back with a look of distaste. None of his other men, standing around the edge of the plateau, moved at all as their companion flailed in agony.

"Roll!" Martina shouted. "Stop, drop, and roll!" But Aloha wasn't listening.

Theo took a step toward the burning man, maybe ready to shove him to the ground and try to slap out the fire. But Aloha was still holding his gun; it swung toward Theo as the man twisted and wailed. Theo dodged to the side as a bullet cracked on the air, and at the same moment Aloha's left heel vanished off the edge of the cliff. He toppled and was gone, his screams lengthening.

Then silence.

Sam felt sick. "What happened?" he whispered, his mouth feeling drier than ever.

"Indeed." Flintlock's gaze, nearly as fierce as the beam of light that was still hitting the stone surface of the door, turned on Sam and Martina. "What *happened*, kids?"

"It's the gnomon," Martina said shakily. She looked as queasy as Sam felt. "It must be some kind of trap. If it's in the wrong position, it focuses the sunlight right here near the door."

"And then . . ." Sam swallowed.

"And then," Martina agreed.

"Take it down," Flintlock ordered, his voice curt.

The men standing around the perimeter of the plateau looked a little uneasy. None of them moved.

"You do it," Flintlock told Sam, Martina, and Theo. "You're the ones responsible for this."

Sam stared. "You want us to *touch* that thing?" They'd just seen the gnomon set a man on fire, and now Flintlock wanted them to move it? The beam of light was still focused on the door like some kind of death ray.

"I believe my instructions were clear," Flintlock answered.

"It's okay, Sam," Martina said. "We just have to stay out of the beam."

"Sure," Sam mumbled. "Fine. We'll just stay out of the way of the killer laser beam."

The three of them grouped themselves carefully around the gnomon. "On three," Theo said softly. "One . . ."

Sam took hold of the smooth glass. Now he had more to worry about than dropping the thing. What if his sweaty hands couldn't keep their grip? What if he or Martina or Theo slipped or stumbled into the light's path?

"Two . . ."

He could still smell burned flesh in the air.

"Three!"

They heaved the gnomon up out of its hole, and the beam of light went out as if flipped off by a switch. Sam let out a huge sigh of relief. As they struggled to lay the wing gently on its side once more, Flintlock walked to the edge of the plateau and glanced over, presumably at the remains of his Hawaiian-shirted henchman. Smoke rose in a narrow wisp.

Flintlock shrugged, turned, and walked silently back toward the three kids.

"You said the *wrong* position?" he demanded, his cold eyes on Martina.

"Yes, that's what . . ." Martina's voice trailed off. "What I said," she finished weakly. "It was wrong."

"*You* were wrong."

Sam didn't think the girl's face could get any paler, but it did. "Yes," she whispered.

Flintlock took in a long breath and let it out slowly, studying her. He reached a hand inside his jacket and pulled out a gun of his own.

"I don't know if you're stupid enough to try and trick me, or if you're really just a kid who's out of her league," he said at last. "But either way—I'm going to make sure that doesn't happen a second time. You." He pointed the gun at Theo. "Stand in front of that door."

Sam jumped forward. "What?" he blurted out. "You can't—!"

Theo held up a hand and shook his head. Slowly, he walked over to stand right where Aloha had stood. His face looked calm and proud, without a trace of fear.

"You're going to try again," Flintlock told Sam and Martina. "And if you're wrong this time, your friend's going to burn."

CHAPTER SEVEN

"No!" Sam shouted. "You can't do this!"

Flintlock pointed toward Martina. "Argue with her, not with me. Much more productive that way. We've already wasted enough time up here, and losing associates of mine makes me very cranky."

Sam's mouth opened and closed. In his mind he could see the flames eating away at the red and orange flowers on Aloha's shirt. He felt like he could still hear the man screaming.

Sam looked over at Theo. Was he going to be next?

Sam walked slowly back toward the sundial and Martina. Now it wasn't just her hands that were trembling.

"I was wrong," she whispered.

"Yeah. It happens." Sam stood staring down at the marks in the rock. Getting stuff wrong—it was a part of solving puzzles. Sometimes you had to guess wrong the first time to be right the second, or the third. But this was a lot more serious than sticking the wrong number in a sudoku.

"He's dead," she choked out. "That guy. He was kind of a jerk, but he died because I was wrong, Sam. And now—"

"Hey!" Sam interrupted her. She was freaking out. This was not good. If they'd ever needed Martina's brain in full working order, it was now. "We *both* got it wrong. But that doesn't mean we'll be wrong again. Listen! We landed that plane, didn't we? We didn't make a mistake then. Right, Marty? Right?"

He knew she was panicking when she didn't immediately say "Don't call me Marty." She just nodded, shivering.

Sam lowered his voice. "Theo needs us," he said. "We'll get it this time."

She nodded again, closed her eyes, and took a deep breath. When she opened them, Sam was relieved to see the familiar know-it-all expression slowly coming back. "Okay," she muttered. "We missed something. What? I know all about history. I'm *sure* I didn't make a mistake with the first of the thirteen colonies. But there's something we didn't think of."

Sam's eyes were on the metal plaque in the ground. "With puzzles, sometimes the most important piece of information looks like it's not important at all."

"You mean, like, the devil is in the details."

Actually, Sam thought, *the devil might be standing over there in a three-piece suit.* "Right," he agreed. "Something that looks insignificant could be the key. We were thinking about the word 'first.' But maybe that's not actually the most important thing in this poem."

He risked a quick glance at Theo, trying to send him a reassuring message with his eyes. *Don't worry. We've got this.*

To his surprise, Theo met his gaze and gave a quick nod. Like he had heard Sam's thoughts and had replied, *Not worried. I trust you.*

Sam looked back down at the plaque, trying to read it with fresh eyes.

THOUGH YOUR CONSTITUTION MAY BE HALE,
YOUR QUEST SHALL BUILD A MIGHTY THIRST.
IF YOU WISH TO ENTER MY OASIS,
YOU MUST FIRST LOOK TO THE FIRST.

"Maybe a broken finger or two would speed up their thought process, boss?" said one of Flintlock's men.

Martina held up a hand, as if the man were simply annoying her with his threats. "Quiet," she said without looking up. Sam was impressed. The girl had gone from freaked out to focused in sixty seconds flat.

"Hale," Martina muttered. "No, that can't be it."

Thirst, Sam thought. Yeah, he was thirsty all right. *Oasis?* That sounded good, but it didn't offer him a clue.

"Constitution?" Martina thought aloud. "Hmm, that just means 'health' or 'condition.'"

"Wait," Sam exclaimed. "What if there's a double meaning, like in a cryptic crossword? What if it also means the Constitution of the United States?"

Martina's face lit up. "Of course!" she exclaimed. "The first! The first state that voted to approve the Constitution!"

"And it was . . . ?" Sam prompted.

"Delaware!" She frowned. "I think."

Sam jumped when a heavy hand fell onto his shoulder and squeezed. "Better hope you're right this time," Flintlock muttered.

Sam swallowed. "You *think*, or you *know*?"

Martina swallowed hard. "I think I know."

"That will have to do," said Flintlock. He pointed to the gnomon. "Try it."

Slowly Sam and Martina bent up the glass instrument again. They both strained, but without Theo's help, they couldn't get it off the ground.

"You. Give them a hand." Mr. Flintlock waved a hand at the man with a penchant for breaking fingers. He sneered as he came across the plateau to help them.

As they lifted the gnomon from the ground, Sam glanced up and saw Theo close his eyes. His lips moved silently. He was ready for whatever was going to happen.

"Oh, Sam . . . ," Martina said.

"We're right this time," he promised her.

"We're about to find out." Flintlock smiled. He pointed his gun at Theo. "Move an inch, big fella, and you're dead anyway."

The spindle slid into place. The glass wing stood upright, beautiful and deadly.

Martina gasped and Sam's heart plummeted as a beam of pure white light sprang from the glass wing and shot toward the door. But Theo didn't make a sound. The beam missed him by two feet, focusing instead on a small crack, about the size of Sam's hand, in the rock next to Theo's head. There was a groaning, grating sound of rock moving against rock—

And like a magic trick, the door behind Theo opened.

It moved like a normal door—How could it *do* that? Where were the hinges?—swinging inward to reveal only darkness beyond.

"Oh, thank you," Martina whispered shakily. "Thank you, thank you."

Sam felt weak with relief. Theo met his eyes and, for a moment, there was the ghost of a smile on his face.

Unfortunately, when Sam flicked his eyes over to Flintlock, he was smiling too. "Good," he murmured, grasping Sam's shoulder with a meaty hand. "Very, very good."

Some of Flintlock's men moved forward a few steps to squint into the open doorway, but Flintlock barked at them to stop.

"Haven't you pinheads ever heard of the canary in the coal mine?" Flintlock sneered. "There might be other traps inside. Send in our little birds first." And with that, he shoved Sam in the back, pushing him in the direction of the mysterious doorway.

So now it was Sam's turn to be a guinea pig? He shot a glare at Flintlock and went to stand at Theo's side, peering into the gloom.

"I can't see a thing," he shouted. "How am I supposed to—"

"Martina's got a flashlight," Theo said suddenly, a little too loud. Sam looked over at him—a question in his eyes. Theo winked.

"Actually, Sam has—" Martina started to say.

Sam knew, he just *knew*, that Martina was about to point out that Sam had his own flashlight in his backpack. He saw Theo give her a sharp warning look. The big guy was definitely up to something.

Martina was annoying, but she was no dummy. She got the point.

"Um . . . ," she faltered, trying to figure out a way to finish that sentence. "Sam has . . . a rare fear of flashlights . . . so I'd better go over there." Pulling out her flashlight, she walked over to join the boys. Flintlock followed, keeping a bit of distance between them, and his men began to gather behind him.

When Martina reached his side, Sam turned to her and muttered, "A *fear* of flashlights? That was the best you could do?"

Martina shrugged. "What? It's a real thing. Selaphobia."

Sam stared at her. "You are truly the weirdest person I have ever met."

Martina held her chin up high. "I will take that as a compliment."

Martina flicked on her flashlight. The beam reached inside the doorway, playing over nondescript rock walls within. "Not much to see," she said.

"Sam." Theo was suddenly right behind him, whispering in his ear. "On my mark, you've got to destroy that glass wing. Whatever it takes. Got it?"

Sam nodded, swallowing hard.

Theo suddenly groaned and doubled over.

"Theo! What's wrong?" Sam shouted, trying to sound as alarmed as he could.

"What's the matter with him?" Flintlock demanded.

"I don't know!" Sam hovered over Theo, hoping he looked worried. He was never very convincing in drama class. Out of the corner of his eye, he saw Theo's fist close over a good-sized chunk of rock on the ground.

A couple of the men behind Flintlock shuffled backward. "I bet it's some kind of poison gas!" one said sharply. "Keep your distance!"

Flintlock frowned, clearly skeptical, and stepped forward to take a closer look at Theo. A second later, Theo snapped upright, driving a fistful of rock into the man's stomach.

"In!" Theo shouted, diving through the doorway. Martina stumbled in right behind him.

As Flintlock fell, Sam grabbed his own rock, whirled, and threw it hard at the gnomon, like a pitcher delivering a fastball. The rock hit its target, shattering it in an explosion of glass and light, and rock ground against rock as the stone door started to swing closed once more.

Flintlock was struggling back to his feet. "Stop them!" he shouted breathlessly, his face ugly with rage and pain. "Stop the *door*!"

"Come on, Sam!" Theo yelled. But before Sam could make it to the doorway, a hand closed around his arm, nearly yanking him off his feet. One of Flintlock's men had grabbed him and was pulling him back out into the open.

Something whizzed past Sam's face, and then Martina's flashlight cracked his captor right on the bridge of his nose. The hand around Sam's arm loosened as the man howled. Sam wrenched free and threw himself back through the narrow slice of doorway, which was growing narrower by the second.

He stumbled straight into Theo, and they both fell hard to the ground, the stone door shutting behind them with a grating *crunch*.

The darkness was thicker than anything Sam had ever experienced before. He couldn't see a thing. He tried to roll off Theo, thumped into a jumble of arms and legs that must have been Martina, seemed to be standing on his own hand for a second—how had *that* happened?—and then staggered upright with a yell of alarm as bright-white light blazed into his eyes, blinding him.

Another trap! Or . . . wait—nope, it was just Martina.

"Sorry," she said, and the light moved away. Blinking, Sam realized that she had a sort of head lamp thing strapped to her forehead, the beam of light bouncing crazily around the cave as she looked around.

"Where did that come from?" Sam demanded. "No, don't turn this way again!"

"My backpack, of course. Weren't you ever a Boy Scout? Always be prepared? Hey, guys—look."

She tilted her head and held it still. The beam from the head lamp fell on the door, and Sam gulped. It wasn't closed all the way. Someone had wedged a rock into the crack, and already fingers were reaching through it, grasping at the air.

"Pull! Put your back into it!" Flintlock's voice boomed.

"It's only a matter of time before they get through," Theo said, rising to his feet. "Let's move."

"Move?" said Sam. "Where? What is this place, anyway?" As they hurried away from the door, Sam tried to get a sense of the place. A narrow tunnel carved out of rough rock, longer than the beam from Martina's head lamp could reach, stretched before them straight into the heart of the mountain.

"Find something to use as a lever!" Mr. Flintlock's voice came faintly from behind them. "Hurry up!"

"An abandoned gold mine, I bet," Theo answered, moving farther into the tunnel.

"That's a good guess," Martina agreed. "Death Valley was part of the Gold Rush, back in the nineteenth century."

"And you look like some kind of old-timey prospector with that thing on your head," Sam told her as they both followed Theo. "If you hadn't had such good aim with that flashlight, I'd tell you how ridiculous it looks."

"Is that actually a Sam Solomon attempt at saying thank you?"

"Come on, you two!" Theo's voice was impatient.

"You think they can really pry that stone door open with their fingernails?" Sam asked, catching up with him. "Those guys looked tough, but not *that* tough."

"That helicopter is almost definitely full of supplies," Theo answered grimly. "Plastic explosives. Detonators. Everything they need. At least that's what I would bring."

Sam blinked. "Of course that's what you would bring, Theo. Because you're just a normal kid who won a contest, right?"

"Sam, he's right," Martina said. "We'd better—"

But Sam had stopped in his tracks. "No," he said sharply. "No! I am not moving from this spot until he tells me what is really going on here."

Theo turned around, frowning, covered in dust and grit from his dark hair to his boots, his head brushing the top of the tunnel. Massive. Like a giant. Or an action hero. Not like any kid Sam knew, that's for sure.

What ordinary kid knew all about detonators and plastic explosives? What ordinary kid wasn't even surprised when a tourist pulled out a gun, and a helicopter full of bad guys showed up?

"What do you mean?" Martina asked. "Why would Theo know any more than we do about these guys?"

"Are you kidding me?" Sam exclaimed. "Look at him! Look at his face! He *knows something*. I bet Evangeline does too. This trip has been a disaster since the moment we stepped on that plane, and Theo is going to tell us why."

"Sam, look—it has been suspiciously insane, but maybe this isn't the best time to talk," Martina said, casting an anxious glance over her shoulder.

"Why did that goon with the Hawaiian shirt act like he knew who we were? What was that crazy sundial puzzle doing in the middle of the desert?" Sam didn't look away from Theo. "Who put it there and made sure it would vaporize anybody who got the answer wrong? Why are we here, Theo?"

Theo studied Sam's face for a few seconds. Sam expected the kid to tell him off, to say he was crazy, maybe even to confess that they really *were* all on some kind of twisted hidden-camera reality show. But what ended up coming out of Theo's mouth was something completely unexpected.

"What do you know about Benjamin Franklin?"

Sam wanted to scream. "Benjamin Franklin?" he spluttered. "Really? Listen, I'm not interested in pop quizzes while I'm inside a pitch-black abandoned gold mine being chased by men with guns! I told you, I want the truth!" Sam stomped his foot on the stone floor for effect.

A moment later, something shifted under his boot, and the ominous sound of stone grinding on stone filled his ears once more.

"Uh-oh," Sam said.

"What's happening?" Martina looked wildly around, sending the light from her head lamp swinging. Just as it settled on what looked like a stone button depressed into the rock floor, Sam felt the ground give way beneath his feet.

And then they fell.

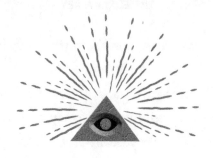

CHAPTER EIGHT

Sam felt a sickening lurch as he dropped into a deep shaft, which must have been hidden under the cave. He flailed, trying to grab on to something, but only managed to crash into a rock wall on one side and Martina on the other. It was no use. He braced for the impact.

But instead of the cold, hard ground, he hit—

Water! Cold water fountained up around him with a splash that rivaled his best cannonball at the neighborhood pool. He had about half a second to be relieved that he wasn't dead before the water closed over his head.

He was sinking. He was drowning!

Sam kicked and struggled, his heavy boots dragging at his legs, his backpack weighing him down like an anchor.

He forced his eyes open, but blackness was all around him, as suffocating as the water. With no sense of direction, Sam had the horrifying realization that even if he could swim, he'd have no idea which way to go.

And then, somewhere nearby, a white light glimmered like a ghost in the darkness.

His chest aching fiercely, Sam shoved the straps of his backpack off his shoulders and struck out for the wavering beam of light that sliced through the water. Martina's head lamp! A few seconds later, he broke through the surface, his breath coming in ragged gasps.

"That head lamp . . . that thing's . . . waterproof?" Sam choked out, kicking hard to keep himself afloat.

"*That's* the first thing you're going to say to me?" Martina spluttered. "How about, 'Gee, Marty, nice to see you're not dead!'" Theo was bobbing beside her, looking a little worse for wear. His dark-brown skin had suddenly gone a pale shade of gray.

"Fine, fine," Sam said, grabbing at a lump of rock sticking out from the wall. "But what the heck is this place? I thought Death Valley was supposed to be dry!"

Martina seized the edge of the wall as well, sucking in several breaths.

"An underground water source, I guess," she panted. "Must have filled up one of the old mine shafts . . . Sam— are you laughing?"

Sam suddenly found himself giggling like a maniac. "An oasis!" he choked out. "Just like that inscription next to the sundial said! Too bad the poem hadn't mentioned we were going to *drown* in it!"

It took a special talent to drown in a desert. He hoped they'd mention it in his obituary.

"Sam!" Martina snapped, and then coughed. She lost her grip and floundered for a moment, then managed to wedge her fingers into a crack. "Get it together!"

"Right. Sorry." Sam gasped, swallowing his laughter along with a mouthful of water that tasted like mud. "It was just—kind of funny. So. Okay." He shook his head, got in a steadying breath, and realized that Martina looked different—and it wasn't just that she was soaking wet. "Hey, Marty, where are your glasses?"

"Where do you think?" Martina shook her clinging hair out of her face. "At the bottom of the mine shaft, probably."

"Can you see without them?" Sam asked.

"I can see you wasting time asking me dumb questions! Forget the glasses for now. We need to find a way out of here!" The light from Martina's head lamp swung around, revealing slick, wet walls high over their heads. No ladder. No rope. Nothing.

"There's no way we can climb the walls," Sam said. "Way too slippery."

"Well, we can't stay here," Martina said.

"No kidding," Sam agreed. "And it's not like anybody's going to show up to rescue us."

"The only people likely to show up . . . are Flintlock and his men," Theo said, a little breathlessly.

"Can't go up, can't stay here," Sam went on. "So we have to go . . ."

"Down?" Martina gazed at the cold, black water all around them.

"Down," Theo said. He took a deep breath and dived.

But he didn't get far before bubbles exploded in a flurry across the water's surface. Theo's head reappeared. His face was twisted with pain.

"Theo!" Martina, who was nearer, grabbed for him.

"No, don't!" Theo pulled away. "My shoulder—don't touch it."

"Give me your other hand," Martina insisted. Theo let her take hold of his left arm, wincing.

"What's wrong?" Sam demanded.

"I think my shoulder's dislocated," Theo groaned. "I tried to break my fall on the way down, but we were dropping too fast. Jerked it out of the joint, I guess . . ."

"So you can't swim?" Sam asked.

Theo's face crumpled. For the first time since they'd met, the big guy actually looked like what he was—a kid. "No," Theo said, his voice heavy with shame. "I guess I can't."

Despite how angry Sam was at Theo for keeping secrets from them, he felt sorry for the guy. "Hey, man. Don't worry—we'll get out of here. Marty, give me that lamp thing." Sam held out his hand for Martina's head lamp.

"It should be me going down there," Theo said.

Sam chuckled humorlessly. "Don't worry," he replied. "Somehow I have the feeling you'll have another chance before this day is done."

Theo nodded. "Be careful," he said, his voice tight with pain.

"Take a couple of deep breaths before you dive." Martina watched as Sam struggled to get the head lamp's strap around his head without letting go of his grip on the wall. "It'll help raise the oxygen levels in your blood."

Sam did as she suggested, then sucked in a huge breath and dived.

Sam's time in the two-hundred-meter relay used to be pretty good. But tearing down the lanes at a nice, clean, brightly lit pool hadn't really prepared him for swimming down into utter blackness in a T-shirt and jeans.

The head lamp's ray pierced the murk like a knife as he swam down, but there was nothing to see but water. He kicked hard, even though his feet in their heavy boots felt clumsy. He would have killed for a pair of flippers. He swam deeper and deeper, but there seemed to be no end to this mine shaft, or to the darkness of the abyss.

Sam was beginning to get disoriented, so he was about to turn back before he lost his bearings when the torchlight bounced off something that wasn't water. Polished stone, maybe? No, it had a metallic shine to it. It was metal—brass. A rectangular brass door had been set into one side of the mine shaft's wall.

Sam stopped swimming, letting the weight of his clothes and boots pull him gently down toward the floor. His chest was starting to ache again. He needed to save enough air to make it back to the surface, so he could only afford to spend a few seconds to get a sense of what was he was dealing with before he had to head back up.

First, the door. A door was good—a door meant a way out. But Sam couldn't see a knob, handle, keyhole—anything. No way to get it open.

His eyes took in what was on either side of the door. On the right, there was a hole as wide as Sam's body, covered by an iron grate. On the left, he saw a three-by-three-foot square etched into the stone. More than a square—a grid. Every little square inside the big one was filled with a number. Every square but three. Those three were blank. And each of the blank squares had a hole in its center.

He knew instinctively that it was another puzzle, like the sundial on top of the mountain. But who in the world was going around creating deadly puzzles in an old gold mine in the middle of a national park? And why?

52	61	4	13	20	29	36	45
14	3	62	51	46	35	30	19
53	60	5	12	21	28	37	44
11	○	59	54	43	38	27	22
55	58	7	10	23	26	39	42
9	8	57	56	41	40	25	24
50	63	2	15	18	31	34	47
16	○	64	49	48	33	32	○

Maybe it's Benjamin Franklin, Sam thought with a semi-hysterical chuckle.

Sam turned the beam of his head lamp to the floor of the tunnel. His backpack was in one corner, and Martina's was nearby. Sam had a moment of grief for his comic books before he was distracted by the sight of a dozen little stone tiles littered all over the floor. Each had a different number and a metal prong sticking out of its back. They looked just the right size to fit into the empty squares on the grid.

Bingo.

The pressure in Sam's chest was tightening, as if someone was turning a screw in his ribs. He was out of time. Planting his feet against the floor, Sam pushed off as hard as he could and shot upward through the water. His vision had just started to cloud from lack of oxygen when he broke through the surface, heaving in huge breaths.

"Well? Did you find anything?" Martina looked over eagerly as Sam grabbed hold of his friendly hunk of rock once more. But she had to wait until he could breathe again for her answer.

"Door," Sam gasped out finally. "But no way . . . to open it. And numbers. A grid on the wall. Like a mega-sudoku kind of thing. With three numbers missing."

"Sudoku?"

Sam nodded. "Yeah, but a lot bigger. And there weren't any repeating numbers like there are in sudoku. They looked random—double digits, single digits—like nothing I've ever seen before. But there's got to be a pattern."

Martina hesitated a moment, a thoughtful look coming over her face. She turned to Theo, hanging onto her shoulder, his face looking even grayer than before.

"You mentioned Benjamin Franklin," she said. "Why?"

"Ben Franklin?" Sam exclaimed. "What is with you two? The Founding Fathers are not going to help us now."

Theo pursed his lips, as if there were a secret resting on his tongue and he wasn't ready to let it out.

"Maybe they are," Martina insisted, giving up on Theo for the moment. "Listen, Franklin developed a puzzle. It was *a lot* like sudoku. He called it a Magic Square of Squares."

Despite himself, Sam was intrigued. "Explain."

"Well, every row and every column in the grid add up to the same number. And there are 'bent-rows' too—diagonals that look like V's, on each side of the grid—they also add up to the same number."

"Okay," Sam said slowly. "Let's say you're right. I still don't understand what the guy on the hundred-dollar bill has to do with some death trap in the middle of—"

Sam's words were interrupted by a huge *boom* that reverberated through the cavern, sending the water around them sloshing and bits of gravel and rock raining down on their heads.

Sam swung the head lamp's light up the mine shaft, but there was nothing to see but dust motes floating through the air. But he didn't need to see anything to guess what had happened.

"Plastic explosives?" he asked Theo, who nodded. The kid's jaw was tight and he was taking in slow, careful breaths, trying to keep his body still in the water.

"Sam!" Martina said, an edge to her voice. "If it's really one of Franklin's magic squares, you need to figure out if the sum of those rows and columns is the same number. It's the only way to solve it."

"Okay," Sam replied. "I'll be right back—don't leave without me."

Martina gave him a halfhearted glare. "Funny."

Sam took another breath and dived.

He could replace the missing numbers. Solve the puzzle. He'd never let a puzzle beat him yet. He could do this.

Right?

Down, down, down—as fast as he could go. Soon the puzzle was in the glow of the head lamp once again.

52	61	4	13	20	29	36	45
14	3	62	51	46	35	30	19
53	60	5	12	21	28	37	44
11	●	59	54	43	38	27	22
55	58	7	10	23	26	39	42
9	8	57	56	41	40	25	24
50	63	2	15	18	31	34	47
16	●	64	49	48	33	32	●

Okay. It was just math. He could do math with his hands tied behind his back. Or, in this case, under a hundred tons of water. In the dark. Sure! After this trip, algebra tests would be like a walk in the park!

He cleared his mind, pushing away the fear so that he could focus on the puzzle in front of him. He quickly added up several rows and columns—twice, just to be sure. Martina was right. They all added up to the same number: two hundred and sixty.

So that number at the bottom of the far-right column should be a seventeen. Sam scrabbled in the tiles beneath him. Seventeen, seventeen . . . there! He shoved the tile into place, forcing the metal prong into its hole. He felt something vibrate inside the stone, like tumblers in a giant lock falling into place.

His lungs were starting to burn. The urge to inhale was fierce, but he fought it. The second missing number, the one closest to the top . . . it had to be six. He'd seen that one as he was looking for the seventeen! He scrabbled in the dirt and had inserted it in five seconds flat.

He was so close to solving it—but his lungs were screaming for air. He had no choice—he had to go back.

When he finally surfaced, he could only cling to the rock wall for a minute or two, choking down breaths, unable to speak.

One more. That was all. He looked up, shaking water out of his eyes. "Listen, guys. I've almost got it. I . . ."

But it didn't look like Theo could hear him. Eyes half shut, he didn't even seem to notice that Sam was there. His head had fallen limply against Martina's shoulder. She hung on to him with one hand, struggling desperately to keep his face above water.

"He passed out a few seconds after you went down," she said, her voice shaking. "I don't know how much longer I can hold him. If we don't get out of here soon . . ." She stopped, as if she didn't like how the sentence might end.

Above, a shout—"We're in!"—echoed off the stone walls. Footsteps on stone. Flintlock and his men had finally broken through the door.

"Better . . . leave me," Theo mumbled without opening his eyes.

"Don't be an idiot," Sam gasped, and dived.

He wanted to tell them that everything was going to be okay—he had only one number left to go—but there wasn't time. Better to save his breath for swimming.

Sam's whole body was angry with him. He was hungry and so tired . . . but he kept pushing his arms through that water, forcing himself deeper and deeper, until he reached the bottom.

Okay—it's go time.

He squinted at the bottom row, where the last number was missing. Even with a brain starved for oxygen, Sam could figure it out. *One!* The last missing number was a one!

Sam pawed through the stone tiles. Over and over he spotted a one—but it was always next to some other number: *41. 19. 12. 81.*

The last tile he needed to solve the puzzle was nowhere to be found.

CHAPTER NINE

Had Sam been wrong? Had he missed something? Made a mistake in his math? Maybe that was why there was no tile with a one on it—because it wasn't the right answer.

Sam had told Martina that everybody got things wrong sometimes.

But not him.

Not now.

He couldn't afford to make a mistake, because with Theo passed out up there, Martina trying to hold on, and scary guys hurrying their way, getting it wrong wasn't just a bad score on a math test. He thought about adding the lines again, but he knew he didn't have the precious seconds.

Tight pressure in his lungs, burning in his throat—it was decision time. Swim back up for one more breath and risk letting all of them fall into Flintlock's hands again? Or stay underwater and keep searching for that missing tile, even if it meant he might never take another breath?

Sam's choice was made before he even realized that he'd made it. In a split second, he was back to pawing through the tiles, turning them over, tossing them aside so that they fell in slow motion through the water.

The number one had to be here. It *had* to be.

Because if it wasn't—he'd blown it. Just like he'd always been afraid that he would. Just like his mom had said at the kitchen table a few days ago. And what had he done? Ignored her. Blood was thumping in his temples, the water waiting to rush into his lungs.

Sure, Sam Solomon could plan pranks and solve puzzles and win contests. That's what he'd always liked best. But study for a math test? No, better to work out how to hack into the vending machine in the school cafeteria and make it spew free Snickers bars all over the floor. Do his homework? Better to spend hours trying to beat his high score on *Hamster Maze*.

Better to use his brain for stuff that didn't really matter that much.

Because what if—when something really *did* matter—his brain just couldn't get the job done?

Sam had turned over every tile he could see. And none of them had a number one.

He'd read about drowning. He knew the physiology. But the only thing he wanted to know now was, *how much will it hurt?*

Just as the last sliver of hope was slipping away, the light of the head lamp caught two lumps on the ground nearby—their backpacks!

One last chance. Sam lunged forward, snagged the strap of Martina's backpack, and yanked it toward him. No tiles under it—though her glasses were there. Sam grabbed his own backpack and dragged it aside.

One lonely tile sat buried beneath it. Sam grabbed it without even looking at the number.

It *had* to be a one. Because if it wasn't, Sam was wrong. Not a puzzle master, just a pawn who'd let his friends down. Also, he was about to die.

The metal prong on the back of the tile slid into place. Sam felt the wall vibrate even before he glanced at the number on the tile.

It was a one.

Before Sam could even register relief, something began to happen all around him.

The water! It was moving!

A fast-moving current swirled through his hair, dragged at his clothes, and tugged him over to the grate in the wall. The water in the mine shaft was being sucked away through the hole like a giant bathtub drain. Sam was pinned face-first against the grate, water roaring in his ears, blinding him. Now he knew what it felt like to be one of those little rubber bath toys he had as a kid.

And he still couldn't breathe. Couldn't breathe. Couldn't *breathe* . . .

Then the pressure let him go, and he felt air on the back of his neck and pouring into his lungs. He was sliding down the wall, and he hit the floor with a soggy *thump*. After a moment, he rolled over onto his stomach, tried to push himself up, and couldn't.

The head lamp had been washed off his head, and Sam was plunged into utter darkness. He was so tired. Maybe he'd just lie here for a while . . .

"Sam. Sam!"

Someone was shaking his shoulder, hard. Sam tried to bat the someone off, but it was difficult to move his arms. *Ow.* He hurt all over.

"Sam, wake up! Don't you die on me!"

It was Martina. Clearly she wasn't going to leave him alone to have a nice little rest. Sam groaned a little and opened his eyes. Martina was bending over him, holding the head lamp, her wet hair plastered over her face.

Sam dragged a breath into his lungs and curled up on his side, coughing and wheezing. He felt like he'd been hit by a truck, but he was alive. And so, crouched against a wall, holding his right arm with his left hand, was Theo.

"You did it!" said Martina. "It was a magic square, wasn't it?"

Sam managed a smile. "It sure was, genius."

They'd survived. That was good.

A voice suddenly boomed down from the top of the mine shaft. "Down here! Get a rope! A long one!"

Or rather, it was good for about five seconds.

It really doesn't seem fair, thought Sam, as he struggled into a sitting position. *I mean, c'mon! Time out! Call the ref!* They'd all survived a fall into a flooded mine shaft, Theo dislocated his shoulder, Sam solved a puzzle underwater—all Flintlock had to do was climb down a rope? Where was the justice in that?

And what was with that metal door? Sam rubbed water out of his eyes. Since he solved the puzzle, he figured the door would just open . . . but it didn't. It just stood there, still shut tight, mocking him.

"Come on, Sam," Martina urged him. Sam groaned one last time and let her pull him to his feet. He spotted her glasses among the tiles at her feet and picked them up, handing them to her as she tugged him over to the door.

"Isn't there a handle? A knob?" she said, after shoving the glasses back on her face. They were a little crooked. She looked kind of like a mad scientist.

"I didn't see anything like that." Sam had to stop to cough again. "And there aren't any hinges on this side. See?

Do you think it's another puzzle? Maybe we have to touch certain parts of it in sequence?"

"Could be," Martina mused. "Maybe it's equipped with a heat sensor?"

Without a word, Theo heaved himself off the wall and came over to join them. He studied the door for a moment. Then he let go of his right arm, placed his left hand flat against the metal, and pushed.

The door screeched and swung inward.

"It's just a door," he said. "You push it." The big guy actually cracked a quick smile before walking through.

Martina and Sam stared after him, openmouthed.

A second later, Martina grabbed her soaking backpack and thrust Sam's at him before dashing after Theo through the door.

Sam stayed behind. He snatched the three stone tiles—the one, the six, and the seventeen—out of their places on the grid.

"What're you doing?" Martina's voice came from the doorway.

"Making it harder for those guys to follow us!" Sam shouted back. It would work too. He felt the wall vibrate, as it had before, and he heard another grinding, shifting noise far away. Moments later, water began to spill out of the metal grate. It was lapping over the tops of Sam's boots by the time he'd followed Theo and Martina through the door and slammed it behind him, tossing the tiles to the floor on his side.

"Let's see them solve the puzzle now!" he said.

There was a metal wheel on this side of the door, the kind Sam had seen in submarine movies. It must have unlocked when he solved the magic square—he just didn't notice because he was so busy drowning at the time. He grabbed it and spun it to seal the door tight again. Then he turned around to see where they had ended up.

Martina had her head lamp back on, and it illuminated a narrow corridor with another door at the far end, twenty feet away. From the pick marks on the wall and the wooden supports lining the passage, Sam guessed this must have been part of the mine as well.

They hurried together along the corridor until they reached the door. This one did have a handle, and Sam put his hand on it.

"Wait!" said Martina. "What if it's another trap?"

"Trap, schmap," Sam said. "How bad could it be?" He turned the handle, pushed through, and gasped—because what he saw on the other side was not what he expected at all.

"Wow," Martina breathed. "It's some sort of workshop!"

The beam from her head lamp danced over desks and shelves and worktables, piled with coils of wire, glass tubes, stacks of books, piles of paper and parchment, machines that seemed to sprout handles and rods and gears the way bushes sprouted leaves. Sam couldn't even being to guess what most of this stuff was for.

Then Sam spied something he *did* recognize—an old-fashioned lamp hanging on the wall. "Hey, Marty! Don't move your head."

"You *know* not to call me that."

"Whatever. Just keep the light there!"

Sam came closer to the lamp. It was even halfway full of oil. If they just had some matches . . .

"Here, Sam."

Something came flying out of the blaze of light that was Martina—a lighter. Waterproof. Sam grinned. He touched the flame to the wick of one lamp, and then to the others he could see along the wall. When he was done, the whole place was aglow with warm, yellow light.

It looked like the workshop of the maddest inventor ever to wield a test tube. And it looked *old*—a couple of hundred years or so. The desk was leather-topped, the furniture like something out of a museum. But what was an antique workshop doing a hundred feet under the Nevada desert?

Sam turned to the only person around who might have a clue. "Okay, Theo." He eyed the big kid, who was leaning against the metal door, gripping his right forearm against his body, his face ashen with pain.

"It looks like we have a few minutes before we're in mortal danger again, so it's time to level with us," Sam told him. "Tell us what's going on."

Theo nodded, his breath coming in short bursts. "Yeah. Okay. I'll try . . ."

"Sit down," Martina said, gesturing to a wooden desk chair nearby. "I'll pop your shoulder back in. Then you'll be good as new."

After Sam and Theo exchanged a slightly skeptical look, Theo lowered himself into the chair.

"Do you really know what you're doing?" Sam whispered in Martina's ear. "The sight of blood makes me, um, a little . . ."

"Oh, calm down, there isn't going to be any blood." Martina waved him off. "You might hear some popping or a crunching noise, but that's it."

"Okay," Sam said, feeling a little queasy.

"Better talk, Theo," Martina told him, her voice level. "It'll take your mind off what I'm about to do."

"Okay." Theo sounded a little queasy himself. Martina's hands began to probe gently at his shoulder. "You were right, Sam. This isn't just a normal trip, and I'm not just another kid who won the contest. Evangeline and I, we're both members of a secret society called the Founders."

Sam felt his jaw drop open. Martina momentarily stopped what she was doing and stared down at Theo.

Sam was shocked that his "he's an undercover secret agent" guess wasn't too far off after all!

"The group has been around since this country was born, its membership passed down from one generation to the next, its secrets guarded with the members' very lives—OW!"

"Sorry," said Martina. "I got a little too excited. Go on."

"Right." Theo drew in a slow, careful breath. "It all started right after the American Revolution. The men behind the Declaration of Independence were scrambling to organize a working government. The nation was still licking its wounds, and everyone was worried about reprisals from Britain. Worried that one day soon, Britain would rebuild its armies and return to take back what was once theirs. Benjamin Franklin worried about this too, but no one knew exactly what ends he went to in order to protect the United States. No one knew, until one day he gathered six of his most trusted colleagues at a secret meeting. James Madison, John Jay, John Adams, Alexander Hamilton, Thomas Jefferson, and George Washington."

The names brought to mind many American history lessons and drawings of serious-looking men on coins and bills. Sam tried to imagine them as real people, meeting in dark rooms, whispering by candlelight.

"Not all those guys liked each other. But they all agreed to meet if it meant protecting the country. Franklin told them . . ."

Martina bent Theo's arm and pulled his elbow gently away from his body. "Try and relax, Theo. Are you ready?"

Theo nodded, still talking, "He told them that he'd invented something. Something powerful. Something terrible. It could be used to defend the United States. But if an enemy got ahold of it, it would be a disaster. So he swore them to secrecy, and—"

Steadily and slowly, Marty pulled Theo's arm above his head, and Sam thought he heard a faint pop. Theo grimaced, but a moment later, he sighed with relief.

"Thanks," he told Martina. "That's better. Lots better."

"Where'd you learn to do that?" Sam asked Martina, a little awed.

"Girl Scouts." Martina pushed her crooked glasses up her nose, looking proud. "I got a badge."

"Okay, back to Ben Franklin," Sam said. "So, he did more than fly kites in thunderstorms, huh, Theo?"

"A lot more," Martina said cheerfully. "For instance, he invented a stove. The Franklin stove! And bifocals. And—"

"Marty. Seriously? Not now."

"Sorry," Martina said, blushing. "Go on, Theo."

Theo got to his feet and rested his head against the metal door, gently rubbing his right shoulder. "Okay. So Benjamin Franklin revealed his invention to each of the six men and swore them to secrecy. Shortly after, they formed a group called the Founders. They made it their mission to keep Franklin's creation completely secret and completely safe. They hid it, and only the seven of them knew where."

"So this thing's been hidden for, what, two centuries?" Sam asked. "What is it, anyway? A bomb, or a gigantic gun, or what?"

"I don't know." Theo shook his head. "Only the seven Founders knew."

"And they're dead, so they're not going to tell us," Sam put in. "They are dead, right? Don't tell me Ben Franklin invented some kind of zombie death ray."

Martina sighed. "Do you think we actually live in a comic book, Sam?"

"Hey, given what's happened today, 'zombie death ray' doesn't seem completely out of the realm of possibility!" Sam exclaimed.

"No zombies, Sam," Theo said with a smirk. "The original Founders died long ago, but their commitment to the cause was passed on. There have always been seven Founders since the days of the Revolution. And they've always protected Franklin's secret with their lives."

Sam felt a chill. He'd wondered what was so important that Flintlock and his men had been willing to kill to get it. Now he knew.

"Once they formed the Founders, the original members made a plan," Theo went on. "They hid Franklin's weapon in a secret vault that could only be opened by someone bearing seven keys. But these weren't just your normal run-of-the-mill keys. Franklin knew any key like that could be copied, its lock picked. Instead, they each chose a special artifact, a one-of-a-kind object that represented the ideals they stood for. These artifacts became the keys to open the secret vault. The Founders all kept a key in their possession, its location unknown to everyone but them. Only on their deathbeds did they reveal its location to someone in their family chosen to take their place as the next Founder."

"So this is . . ." Martina looked around, wide-eyed. "This is the hiding place for Ben Franklin's key?"

"Yes," said Theo.

"Seriously?" Sam frowned. "Somebody built all this just to hide a key? Sundial puzzles and crazy killer sudokus and . . . and everything? Didn't they have safety deposit boxes back then? This is baloney, guys. And you accuse *me* of living in a comic book!"

Theo looked straight at him. "Why do you think all this is here, Sam? Somebody went to a lot of trouble to build it, to keep it secret. Is my story really so unbelievable, compared to everything you've seen?"

"Let's say you're telling the truth," Martina said. "Why would it be in Death Valley? Ben Franklin never came here! Nevada wasn't even part of the United States when he was alive!"

"Right," said Theo, his face darkening. "Thought you might bring that up, Martina. It happened during the Civil War. One of the Founders of that time betrayed the others. It was . . . a difficult time for the country. Americans against Americans. Anyway, with some of the locations of the keys compromised, the other Founders decided they had to take precautions. Many of them were moved to places like this. Places no one would ever think to look."

Remote, Sam thought. *Sure, like in the middle of the desert. That must have seemed safe to people back in Civil War days. They couldn't have imagined busloads of tourists or helicopters of bad guys in the middle of Death Valley.*

And yet . . . here they were.

"So . . . wait a minute." Sam looked at Theo. "You *knew* this place was here, in Death Valley?"

Theo nodded.

Sam felt his temper heating up. "You took us out here . . . on purpose? You knew what was going to happen?"

"We were looking for this vault, yes. And we knew that there was a possibility that the enemy might catch up with us. But my task was to stay with you and to protect you from harm." Theo couldn't meet Sam's eyes when he said that—as if he thought that he hadn't done a very good job with the protecting part.

"So what does that make you? A Founder? A descendant of . . . whom? Benjamin Franklin?"

"No." Theo shook his head. "That's Evangeline. Her ancestor, Richard Temple, was the illegitimate son of Benjamn Franklin. Franklin never claimed Temple in public, but he secretly passed the torch of the Founders on to him when he died."

Sam ran a hand through his wet hair. Skinny, frozen-faced Evangeline Temple was a living descendant of Benjamin Franklin, one of the most important figures in the nation's history? Sam shook his head, trying to get all these new facts to rattle into place inside his brain. "Okay," Sam blurted. "Fine. Evangeline's a Franklin. Why not? So, what about you?"

Theo shook his head. "Who I am isn't important right now. What's important is that we keep as far ahead of Flintlock and his goons as we can."

"So, Flintlock knew this vault was here too?" Sam demanded.

"Doubtful. They must have been following us. Waiting for us to find it first so they could close in."

"And we did." Sam felt his mouth twist in disgust. "Led them right to it. We even opened the door for them."

"We didn't have much choice."

"But why now?" Martina asked. "We're the only people who've been in here for more than a century, right? Why are you looking for this place *now*?"

"Because somebody talked. Someone broke the secret pact." Theo looked away from them, out over the jumbled laboratory, his expression grim.

"Who?" Sam asked.

Theo paused for a couple of seconds. "Evangeline's father."

"Whoa . . . wait," said Sam. "Is he a Founder too?"

"He was."

Sam swallowed hard.

"He disappeared months and months ago," Theo continued. "When Evangeline finally found him, he only had a few moments left. Which is why she had to take his place and make some very quick decisions. It was the first clue that the Founders were under attack once again."

"How did he die?" Martina asked nervously, as if she didn't really want to know.

"Unpleasantly," said Theo. "Let's just say his captors didn't give him much choice but to talk. And even then, he only told them the general location of the key, not how to get into the vault or survive its challenges."

"Oh, man . . . ," Sam whispered.

"The contest," Martina broke in. "That's why Evangeline created this contest, isn't it? You needed someone who could figure out the puzzles."

"Correct," Theo agreed. "Not her first choice, as you'd imagine. But the other Founders have become . . . a little lazy in the past fifty years. Many of them figured those secrets were so dusty and forgotten that no one would ever make a move to steal them ever again. They were wrong."

"Clearly," Sam agreed.

"Anyway," Theo continued, "when Evangeline tried to contact them about the danger, many of them were impossible to contact. Others thought Evangeline must be exaggerating about the danger. In the end, only one came to her aid." Theo looked away, as if recalling a bad memory. But as quickly as the emotion came, Sam watched him push it aside. He continued, "But . . . one person's help wasn't enough. So she came up with the idea of the American Dream Contest. And believe me, Evangeline was less than pleased to find out the top two winners were kids, but there was nothing she could do. We needed you."

Martina frowned. "You could have told us."

"Correction," said Sam. "You *should* have told us. I told my mom the trip was safe! Educational, even! And now I'll be lucky if I get home with all my limbs intact!"

"We didn't know if we could trust you yet," Theo murmured.

"But you do now?" Martina asked.

Theo turned to look at her, rubbing his right shoulder with his left hand. "Yeah. I do."

"Gosh, that's nice," Sam said, scowling. He felt anger pulling into a hard knot in the middle of his chest. "I'm touched."

A deep *thump* echoed through the chamber, making the rock walls tremble. Martina gasped; Sam jerked upright. The metal door vibrated behind Theo's back but held firm.

"Flintlock." Theo got to his feet. "He must have found another way to drain the water."

"But he can't open the door . . . right?" Martina asked, eyeing the metal door nervously. "We locked it from the other side."

"No, but he can blow it up," Theo answered. "We've got to keep moving."

"Right," Martina agreed. "Sam, let's— Sam?"

Sam stood with his arms crossed and a scowl on his face. "You trust us now," he said to Theo. "But maybe we don't trust *you*." He marched right up to the big guy and tried to ignore the fact that he only came up to Theo's chin. "You lied to us," Sam went on. "You said this was a vacation, a sightseeing trip—a prize! And now people are trying to kill us. All because you needed some puzzles solved!"

Theo still couldn't meet his eyes.

Another loud *thump* shook the room.

"Sam!" Martina hissed. "I get your point, but maybe this isn't the time for arguing?"

Finally, Theo looked up. "Look, I'm sorry to have dragged you both into this, I am. But Franklin's secret is more important than any single life. The original Founders all knew that."

"Don't you think you should have let us decide for ourselves?"

"Let's argue about it when we get out of this room!" Martina said. "There has to be a way out somewhere . . ."

"You're right," Theo said, still meeting Sam's stare.

"I am?" Sam blinked.

"There's another door down there." Theo nodded toward the far end of the room, and before Sam could react, he was walking between tables and desks to check it out.

Sam would have loved to knock Theo's shoulder back out of joint, but the big guy had a point. They needed a way out of Ben Franklin's workshop, and they needed it fast.

The door looked familiar once Sam got there—exactly like the one he'd opened by solving Franklin's magic square. A smooth bronze rectangle, flush with the wall, with no handle, knob, or visible way to open it.

"Another puzzle?" Martina asked.

"Has to be," Theo answered. "Something in here will get it open."

Martina quickly moved to start searching one side of the room. Sam turned away from Theo to search the other. He riffled through blueprints, sketches, and maps, glanced at a wooden tray full of little metal letters, scanned shelves full of glass jars with murky contents and dusty labels. He saw tools arranged neatly on oiled cloths—hammers from sledge to tack, pliers big enough to take out a giant's tooth and small enough to pick fleas off a mouse, and every size in between.

It was all very interesting—kind of like sorting through someone else's house—but unfortunately there was nothing that looked anything like a puzzle.

Martina was probably making lists in her head, checking things off, trying to use logic. But logic was going to be too slow. Sometimes you just had to let your mind drift and allow instinct to take over.

Ben Franklin had left a clue here, and Sam was going to find it.

He picked up a small sack made of soft fabric. Something inside it jingled.

"What did you find, Sam?" Martina appeared at his side as Sam emptied the sack out on top of a pile of old papers. Coins.

Sam had been ready to see gold doubloons or glimmering rubies. A pile of dull copper coins was pretty disappointing—but apparently not to Martina.

"Fugio cents!" she exclaimed. "They were the first coins minted after the Revolution!"

"Just pennies? Ugh, figures," Sam said. He picked one up and looked at it. On one side of the thing was a sundial (so *that's* where that puzzle came from!) and on the other side was a chain wrapped around the words "We Are One."

"No gold? Jewels? Pirate's treasure?"

"Do you know how much one of these is worth, Sam?"

"Um . . . a penny?" Sam said as he tossed one into the air.

"Maybe a thousand dollars."

"Seriously?" Sam fumbled to catch the coin before it fell to the ground.

"Yeah, well, money isn't going to help us if we're dead!" Martina said. "Keep looking!"

Sam slipped a couple of pennies into his pocket. A souvenir of the trip of a lifetime. Possibly a very short lifetime.

He stopped at the back of the room to look at a fancy wooden table with a latched lid. Curious, Sam flipped open the latch and lifted the lid to find something so weird he didn't even know what to make of it. Inside, there were a series of glass bowls, all different sizes, each rim painted a different color. The bowls were threaded onto a spindle that ran the length of the table. Each bowl nested inside a slightly larger one, making the contraption look sort of like a huge glass unicorn horn. Under the table Sam found a foot pedal, like one for a piano or a sewing machine. Sam reached out one foot and began to pump the pedal up and down to see what would happen.

The spindle began to turn. And the glass bowls spun slowly around, their colored rims catching the light. Sam reached out to touch one of the bowls. Its red rim squeaked under his damp finger, and a ghostly sound filled the room.

It was something between a church organ and the chime of a bell, strange and beautiful at the same time.

All of a sudden, a loud, grinding noise interrupted the haunting melody. It sounded as if somewhere enormous rusty metal gears had slowly begun to turn.

"Sam!" Martina yelled. "What did you do?"

"Me? What? I didn't do anything!" Sam jumped away from the table and looked wildly around. "Why would you just assume that I— Oh, boy."

Martina followed Sam's gaze, looked up, and shrieked.

The ceiling was moving. Slowly but surely it was easing downward.

It wasn't so much a ceiling, Sam realized, as an enormous slab of stone that had been suspended above their heads, fitting neatly between the four walls but not actually joined to them. The note he'd played on that strange contraption must have triggered something, and now the slab was inching down toward them, getting closer by the second.

If they didn't stop it soon, they'd be crushed.

"Man, Ben," Sam murmured, as if the ghost of Benjamin Franklin could somehow hear him. "You were a genius, all right—but you sure had a twisted sense of humor."

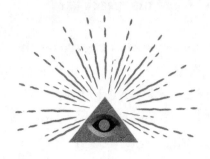

CHAPTER TEN

"Sam! What did you touch?" Martina appeared at his elbow.

"Just this thing!" Sam flapped his hands frantically at the glass bowls/spindle/foot pedal contraption. "It played a note when I touched it."

The ceiling continued to rumble toward them. Another three feet and they'd have to start ducking.

"It's an armonica!" Martina said, staring over Sam's shoulder.

"Not a harmonica!" Sam told her. "This weird glass thing."

"A *glass armonica*, you moron! That's what it's called. Benjamin Franklin invented it." Rock dust showered down on them from above. "You can play different notes on it by touching different bowls. And when you played it . . ."

"I started the ceiling coming down like some giant trash compactor?"

"Yes. Yes, you did."

Sam looked up. Theo probably could have reached up and touched the ceiling by now if he stood on his tiptoes. "Okay." He rubbed his hands over his head, as if that would get his thoughts working more quickly. "Don't panic."

"*I'm* not." Martina glared at him.

"I just meant—don't yell at me. No, wait a minute." Back up on top of the mountain, Flintlock had said something—that Sam and Martina solved problems by arguing. "Yes, yell at me! I played the wrong note. Now the ceiling's coming down. So if I play the *right* note, the ceiling should stop. Right?" Sam stretched out a hand.

"Don't touch it!" Martina shouted. "You could make the ceiling come down *faster!*"

"Okay, okay! I won't touch it!" Sam said. "We just have to figure out which note to play."

"Sounds like a puzzle," Theo said quietly. He'd come up behind them without Sam noticing. He sure walked softly for a guy who could probably bench-press a piano.

"Yeah," said Sam. A puzzle where, once again, a wrong answer meant certain death. "There must be clues," Sam muttered. "A puzzle always has clues."

Martina had her nose an inch away from the armonica. "What's this? On the base." She blew dust away from a metal plate, and Sam leaned over her shoulder to look at it: IN MEMORY OF THE BATTLE OF YORKTOWN, 1781.

"Yorktown. That was the last battle of the Revolutionary War," Martina said.

"Okay. Keep talking." Sam couldn't believe those words were coming out of his mouth, but they were. "What do you know about Yorktown?" Martina screwed up her eyes in thought, consulting the giant database that was her memory.

Sam glanced up nervously. The ceiling had come down another inch—it was now about seven feet off the ground. Now Theo *could* touch it. Laying his hands flat against the descending roof, Sam saw him strain, looking for all the world like Atlas holding up the Earth. For a mad second, Sam dared to hope that superhuman Theo could do it, but then his elbows kinked. "Nope," muttered Theo through gritted teeth. "I can't stop it. I'll get something to try to hold it up. You two keep thinking!"

"Um . . . well, Yorktown's in Virginia," Martina told Sam. "The British built a fort there, and the Americans had it under siege. Lord Cornwallis was commanding the British, and they couldn't hold out. Cornwallis surrendered and gave up his sword."

"To George Washington," Theo added over his shoulder. He'd gotten ahold of a metal rod and jammed it into the narrow gap between the ceiling and the wall. It held for a few seconds before the metal crumpled in a shower of sparks. Sam started flipping through the papers in an old rolltop desk.

Martina nodded, impressed. "Right! That was the end of the fighting. The Americans knew they had won."

All of that is great, Sam thought. *But it still isn't music.* "What are we supposed to do?" he asked. "Anyone know Franklin's favorite tune?" Though the ceiling was still over their heads, they were all crouching, Sam noticed. He tugged out a desk drawer and emptied it onto the ground. Then he saw it.

A piece of yellowed paper covered in musical notation. He waved it at Martina. "How about this?"

Theo came over, his eyes running over the page. He whistled seven little notes, and a huge smile broke across Martina's face. She clapped her hands. " 'Yankee Doodle'!" she said. "The British originally made it up to make fun of the Americans, but then the revolutionaries reclaimed it. The American military band played it at Yorktown when Cornwallis gave up his sword!"

Theo grabbed the score. "I knew old Ben wouldn't leave us in the lurch!"

"Oh yeah, big help," said Sam. "Unless we didn't happen to find it and got squashed like roadkill instead!" Sam was already pumping the foot pedal under the table, getting the bowls of the armonica up to speed again.

"Sam, can you read music?" Martina asked.

Sam shrugged. "I played drums for a bit, but the neighbors complained."

"So, no?" said Martina, her face going pale. "Neither can I."

They both turned to Theo. "I've taken a few piano lessons," he said quietly.

Sam raised an eyebrow. Theo, taking piano lessons? He tried to imagine Theo's huge form hunched over a keyboard, tinkling away at Mozart. This day just got weirder and weirder.

"What?" Theo asked, seeing the look on Sam's face. "My mom loved the piano. I did it for her."

"All right, Ludwig van Theo," Sam said, making way for him. "Play away!"

Theo placed the old sheet of parchment on the table behind the armonica and cracked his knuckles. "Knowing the notes isn't enough," he muttered. "You have to be able to play the instrument as well." He licked a finger and reached out to a spinning bowl. The glass squeaked a sour note.

Sam looked up, craning his neck awkwardly. He felt half-crushed already, as if the air itself, compacted by the stone slab over their heads, was pressing down on him.

Theo shook his head. He tried again. "It's not just picking the right bowls," he muttered. "It's the pressure. Have to get it right . . ."

Crack! A lamp shattered on one wall, splattering hot oil onto the floor.

"Hate to rush you, Theo," Sam whispered, "but . . ."

Theo was frowning, concentrating. "No, that's F-sharp, I need C-natural . . ." His fingers jumped over to a new bowl. The sound that squeaked out sounded like some kind of operatic rodent. Sam winced.

"Try again," Martina said, keeping her voice impressively calm.

Theo did. He was bending his knees all the time, dropping farther into a crouch. More notes squealed and shrilled. None of it sounded like music.

"Stuck a feather in his cap and called it macaroni," rattled through Sam's head, fast and high-pitched, maddening and menacing. Theo kept trying. A tall contraption of glass tubes and brass wire on one of the tables groaned and shattered as the ceiling inched lower and lower.

"Don't stop pedaling, Sam," Martina whispered. "Theo, you can do it. 'Yankee Doodle went to London . . .'"

Martina had a pretty good voice, right on key. Sam chimed in, trying to follow her, even though the music teacher at school had begged him to stand in the back row and move his mouth silently when the holiday concert came around.

"'Riding on a pony . . . ,'" Sam and Martina chorused.

Theo picked a new bowl. His thick finger pressed down lightly, then harder. His eyes widened. "That's it!" he said. "Middle C!"

"Keep going!" Martina whispered.

Theo had the hang of it now. His eyes were half on the sheet music, half on the bowls, and as his fingers leaped from one bowl to another, an eerie, piercing music sprang out. The sound was seriously weird, but Sam could recognize the tune. If aliens had decided to invade while whistling "Yankee Doodle," it would have sounded like that.

The ceiling shuddered, paused, and began to rise again. Theo stood up straighter. Sam groaned with relief, and Martina put her hands to her face.

Sam heard other voices, muffled by the thick rock walls. "What's going on in there? Is that music?"

The metal door at the far end of the room swung silently open.

"Come on!" Theo shouted to Sam and Martina.

Sam looked back at the room. Everything more than five feet from the floor was smashed to smithereens. Then he followed the other two through the door. As he swung it shut behind himself, it closed with a thump that he felt in his bones. He got a glimpse of a long passageway just before the door shut, and then darkness closed around them, thick and stifling.

"Marty? Where's your old-timey-prospector head lamp thing?" Sam groped around for her and touched something soft—her hair?

"Sam, get your finger out of my eye! Let me turn it on—there!"

The light sprang on, illuminating the long tunnel Sam had glimpsed earlier.

"Better keep moving." Theo started off, with Martina following. "Flintlock's probably in the workshop right now."

"Trying to figure out the armonica," Martina added.

"Maybe if we're lucky, he'll be tone-deaf." The air felt heavy and damp in his mouth, hard to breathe, as if it were too old.

"Can't count on luck," Theo countered from up ahead. "Let's go."

The light from the head lamp flickered, then died, leaving them in utter darkness again. "Huh," Sam said, stopping abruptly. "So much for luck."

"And moving," Theo added from somewhere next to Sam. "Is it broken?"

"No, I don't think so," Martina's voice said. "It's just the battery."

Sam groaned. "That's not any better, is it? Unless you happen to have a spare battery somewhere on you."

The sound of a zipper rang out. "Of course I have a spare," Martina said with dignity. "Several."

"Of course you do." Sam stifled a grin. Then he remembered that Martina couldn't see him, and he grinned all he wanted to.

"Is that a complaint I'm hearing?"

"Nope, no complaining here!" Little rustling sounds reached Sam's ears as Martina dug through her backpack. Then came a click as the new battery snapped into place.

"Martina?" Theo's voice drifted back; he sounded as if he'd moved ahead a few paces. "You got that light coming? Because the tunnel gets wider up here. I think I found something."

"One second," Martina called.

Light burst out of the head lamp again, casting Theo's shadow across yet another metal door.

Sam peered over Martina's shoulder. "Man. Those Founders just loved doors, huh?" he grumbled.

The tunnel widened out around them, forming a natural cave about as wide as a city street. An arch had been carved in one wall, and a thick iron door blocked it. Right in the middle of the door, a half circle of metal stuck out like a handle. Theo was already tugging on it, but the door didn't budge. Sam ran to his side and lent his own strength. Even between them it was impossible.

Okay, fine. What had I expected? Sam glowered at the doorway. *Bring it on, Ben!* They'd figured out the sundial, the magic square, and the Yankee Doodle of Death. He'd like to see this door stop them now.

"Clues. Always with the clues," he said, mostly to himself. "Theo, move back, okay?" The big guy stepped aside. Sam couldn't see any numbers or letters or even musical notes on the door or the walls near it. But there was the thick metal loop sticking out, and now Sam spied a square metal plate in the floor maybe twelve feet away from the door, with an identical loop jutting up from it.

The plate had wires soldered to it. Sam followed the path of the wires with his eyes. Martina must have been doing the same thing, because the light from her head lamp swung along the wall of the cave until it landed on the thing that the wires were attached to—a metal box, about as tall as Sam himself, with a hand crank on one side.

Sam reached out to touch the crank.

"Wait!" Martina yelled. "Be careful!"

Sam paused with his hand on the old piece of metal. "What? I just want to see what this does."

"Like you did with the armonica?" Martina asked. "Which almost got us all killed?"

"Fine." Sam pulled his hand back. "You come up with an idea, then. How are we going to get through that door? Don't you think this crank has something to do with it?"

"I never said it didn't." Martina pressed her lips together, looking hard at the metal box and at Sam. "I just said be careful. *Think* before you start fooling around with things."

"How long do you want to take to think? Until Flint-lock blows a hole through that last door?" Sam shook his head. "Look around, Marty. There's nothing else to try. All we've got is a metal cube and a crank. So I'm turning the crank." He grabbed hold of the crank, ignoring Martina's look of reproach, and pulled hard. Rusty metal groaned, and the thing began to turn.

The machine started to hum. Sam recognized the sound. He'd heard it a million times—from a refrigerator, a computer, an air conditioner.

Martina recognized it too. "Electricity! It must be some sort of mechanical generator."

"Of course!" Sam kept turning the handle. "This place is all about Ben Franklin, right? Everybody knows about Ben Franklin and the key and the kite! Of course there's a puzzle using electricity!"

"What kind of a puzzle, though?" Martina was look-ing around. "Stop cranking for a minute so we can think. The generator makes electricity when somebody turns the crank, but where does the electricity go?"

"Along those wires," Theo said, pointing at the wires that stretched from the metal box to the square plate on the floor.

Sam let go of the crank and stepped back. "Okay, but that doesn't get us anywhere. The thing about electricity is, it likes to travel in loops. Circuits."

"Oh, you were listening in science class?" Martina asked.

"No, I was listening to my mom after I stuck a fork in an electrical socket." He cast his mind back to that day, years ago, when he'd given himself a good zap and his mom explained what happened. When you plugged something—say, a lamp—into a socket and flipped a switch, it completed a circuit. Then the electricity could travel up the cord and into a light bulb, make the filament glow white-hot, and then travel back down. If the electricity didn't have a cord to travel along, it would use anything that came in handy—like a fork in Sam's hand, and then the rest of Sam's body. Which was why he had promised to never, ever do that again.

"We have to make a circuit," Sam said, finishing his thought. "Join up the generator to the door. I bet that'll open it."

"With what, though?" Martina asked. "It has to be something that will carry a current of electricity. Like wire, or metal, or—"

"How about this?" Theo grunted, staggering back into the glow of Martina's head lamp.

He was dragging something along the floor—a huge metal oval. A link. For a chain.

"Yes!" Sam broke into a grin. He'd been right once again. Sam Solomon: four; Ben Franklin: zero. *You're making this too easy, old guy.* "Where'd you find it?"

"Nearly tripped over it while we were climbing up that tunnel. I didn't realize it was important." Theo dropped the link by the generator. "There's more."

"Here's another one!" Martina shouted.

Martina used her head lamp to hunt down the links, then stood next to each one until Sam or Theo arrived to drag them to the door. It was backbreaking work. Theo could heave one of the links up onto his shoulder and stagger back with it, but it was quicker to drag them. Sam had no choice—dragging was all he could manage.

He'd done two to Theo's five, and he was working on his third when Martina stopped him. "Hey, do you still have that Fugio cent?" she asked.

"If you wanted one, you should have grabbed one of your own," Sam grunted.

"Just give it to me."

Sam didn't have breath to spare for arguing. He dug in his pocket for the little copper coin, handed it to Martina, and went back to dragging.

Martina stood still in the tunnel, the light from her head lamp focused on the coin in her hand.

"It wouldn't . . . kill you . . . to help me out here," Sam pointed out, dumping his link by the generator.

"Look at this," she said, ignoring his comment.

"Helping?" Sam asked. "Remember helping?"

"I *am* helping," Martina answered. "Look!"

Sam went over to look at the penny, glad for the chance to rest his aching back and throbbing arms.

"See this chain?" Martina pointed to the picture on one side of the old coin. "Made of links?"

"Yeah. I see." Sam rubbed his sore hands. "They look like miniature versions of these big ones."

"That's right. And there are thirteen links shown on the coin. I bet we need to find thirteen here in the tunnel."

Sam nodded, counting up the ones they had already connected. "Looks like we've got five to go, then!"

With Sam and Martina both dragging one link, they could nearly keep up with Theo. The fact that he'd had a dislocated shoulder not long ago didn't seem to slow him down.

"Franklin designed the Fugio cent himself, you know," Martina chattered as they dragged.

"Uh." Sam grunted his answer.

"Thirteen links in the chain, you see. The number thirteen was a big deal to him. Thirteen colonies, of course. But he also had a list of thirteen virtues that he lived by."

"Hey, watch it. My toe. Watch out for my toe!"

"Temperance, Silence, Order, Resolution . . ."

"Over there." Sam pointed. "There's another one."

"Frugality, Industry, Sincerity, Justice . . ."

"Pull. *Harder*."

Theo tugged the eleventh link of chain past them, and Sam caught the look of amusement on his face. It was all fine and good for Theo. He wasn't stuck carrying chains with Martina.

"Moderation, Cleanliness, Tranquility, Chastity, and . . . and . . . there's one more. I can't remember it. Shoot. I know there's one more."

"Wasn't one of those virtues 'silence'?" Sam asked.

"Yes."

"So how come you're still talking?"

Martina scowled at him but shut up at last, and between them they hauled the twelfth link over to the pile that they had heaped up between the generator and the door. According to Martina and the Fugio cent, there should be one more somewhere.

"Sam, you start fastening up the links," Theo suggested. "Martina, bring the light and we'll look for the last one."

Left alone, fumbling in the near dark, Sam heaved the links of chain into place, connecting them like the world's largest necklace. This would be much easier with Martina and her light.

"Hey, guys?" he said. "I could use a hand here?"

"Still looking," said Martina from farther up the tunnel, her head lamp bobbing.

Finally, as he was hooking up the twelfth link, he heard their footsteps approaching.

"Last one?" Sam looked up, squinting in the glare of Martina's head lamp.

"There aren't any more," Theo reported.

"What?"

"We can't find the last one." Martina sounded worried. "We must have missed something."

"Well, maybe there *are* only twelve. Maybe it'll stretch." He crouched down to heave them all into position. "Help me."

It was a couple of minutes before they laid all the links out as far as they'd go, but when they were done, they were still a couple of feet short of joining the loop on the door.

"C'mon, pull!" said Sam. "We can make it!"

"No," Martina said. "There *has* to be thirteen. It doesn't make sense otherwise."

"The chain doesn't *have* to be thirteen links long." Sam shook his head. "It just has to be long enough to reach the door."

"Sam, how much do you know about history?"

"Marty, how much do you want to get out of here?"

"We have to get this right. Remember"—Martina gulped—"what happened on the top of the mountain? When we were wrong?"

Remember? Sam wasn't likely to forget a guy bursting into flames, even if it was a guy he didn't particularly like. "Yeah. But, Marty . . ."

"I *told* you not to call me that!"

"Come on!" Sam's voice cracked with impatience. "We can't just stand here and argue all day! We've got to try!"

"Like you tried with the armonica? You nearly got us all killed!"

"Not really fair," Theo spoke up. "Sam couldn't have known what would happen."

"Thank you!" said Sam, slightly surprised.

"But we can't just try stuff randomly," Martina said. "We have to *think it out*. You like sudoku puzzles, right, Sam? What happens if you get careless and put in one wrong number? You lose any chance of getting the rest of the puzzle right. Maybe the same thing could happen here. We've got to get this *right*! And thirteen is *right*!"

"You always think you know best! Martina Wright is always right!" Sam snapped. "You've got the facts, you've done the research, you're a walking Wikipedia! Good for you! But when are you actually going to *do* something instead of standing there arguing with me?"

Sam waited for Martina to yell back.

But she didn't.

"Not really fair either," Theo said into the silence.

Martina was staring down at the links of chain that lay like a clunky metal snake along the floor, her shoulders slumped. "The thirteenth virtue," Sam heard her whisper, her voice sounding louder as it echoed off the stone walls all around.

Then she straightened up, her voice oddly level. "I remember now. Start cranking the generator, Sam."

"What?" Sam stared at her. "Why should I? The circuit isn't finished. It won't do anything. The electricity has nowhere to go."

Sam saw her face flush with anger. "Just do it! You wanted to stop arguing—so stop!" She took a deep breath. When she met Sam's eyes again, she looked more serious than Sam had ever seen her. "Trust me," she said.

Sam looked at Theo. Theo shrugged.

"Okay," Sam agreed. He grabbed the handle of the generator and yanked.

After a few turns, he heard the humming start up. He turned the crank faster.

Martina walked slowly away from him until she was right next to the door. The end of the chain lay at her feet.

"Don't stop cranking, Sam. No matter what happens."

Martina took hold of the metal loop in the doorway. Then she leaned down toward the chain that lay on the ground.

"Marty! Stop! Don't touch that!" Sam called out. What did that crazy girl think she was doing? Didn't she realize that electricity was surging through that chain?

"Martina!" Theo shouted. "*No!*"

She ignored them. Her free hand was trembling as she closed it over the twelfth metal link.

Martina's body shook as if she were a puppet with a madman yanking at the strings. Sam snatched his hand away from the generator's handle, but to his horror, the handle continued to whirl around under its own power, too fast now for him to stop without breaking his fingers.

Rusty metal squealed, and a crack of light blazed between the cave wall and the edge of the iron door as it swung open.

Martina dropped to the floor as if the puppeteer had tossed her away, and lay there—still as death.

CHAPTER ELEVEN

Sam threw himself down at Martina's side. Theo was already there, stripping off her backpack and sliding a hand beneath her neck, turning her body face up. Her eyes were half-open, but she didn't seem to be seeing anything. Her mouth was slack. Sam smelled burned hair. Theo grabbed her wrist, feeling for a pulse.

Sam felt sick. Just a moment ago, he'd been yelling at Martina for talking too much—and now she might never speak again. "Marty," he murmured, shaking her by the shoulders. "Wake up, Marty. You did it. You got the door open. We can get out of here." She didn't move. "Marty!" Sam repeated, shouting now.

"She might need mouth-to-mouth," Theo said.

"Really?" Sam gulped. But this was not a moment to wimp out. "Okay. Mouth-to-mouth. Right."

Sam licked his lips and bent to get closer to Martina's face. *It's just like health class,* Sam told himself. *Except this time it's not a dummy. Well, Martina is a dummy for electrocuting herself in the first place!* Sam scolded himself. *She saved you. She saved your life and opened that door. The least you could do is try to save hers!* "Okay, here I go." He cupped Martina's chin with one hand and held her nose with the other.

"Sorry, Marty," he whispered, leaning close to her face. He sucked in a deep breath, opened his mouth, and—

"Sam?"

Martina's eyes had flipped open. She was staring straight at him, and she looked just as panicked as Sam felt, finding his face two inches from hers.

"Who do you think I am, Sleeping Beauty?" she said, recoiling. "What do you think you're doing?"

"Just trying to save your life!" Sam replied. "Some thanks I get for that!"

"Oh," Martina said, sitting up shakily. "Yeah. Thanks."

"What were you thinking, Marty?" Sam asked. "That was crazy. You could have been toast. Actual toast."

Martina leaned back against the cave wall. Her hair still drifted spookily through the air, as if alive. But her voice was steady. "I was thinking about the thirteenth virtue."

"The what?"

"Remember? I started telling you about it while we were moving the links. Benjamin Franklin had a list of thirteen virtues. Like the thirteen links of the chain."

"Right, but we only found twelve."

"Exactly. Because the thirteenth virtue is Humility. You know, not thinking you're better than anybody else. Or that you know everything."

Sam blinked in astonishment. Was Martina Wright actually blushing?

"Franklin said people should try to 'be like Jesus and Socrates,'" she went on. "Sacrificing themselves for the common good. So I thought that might be the answer. To complete the puzzle, one person had to be humble enough to risk her own life so that the others might go on. She had to realize that her own well-being wasn't as important as the quest itself."

Whoa. Sam shook his head, amazed. Martina had more guts than he'd ever imagined.

"Like you did in that mine shaft, Sam. You risked drowning to save us all. I thought you *had* drowned, for a minute. I was so scared you were dead. So I thought— maybe I could be as brave as you were. Maybe that's what Benjamin Franklin would have expected me to do."

Sam couldn't think of a single word to say.

"Socrates said, 'The only thing I know, is that I know nothing,'" Martina went on, her voice trembling. "I act like a know-it-all sometimes, it's true. Like I've got all the answers. But I want to *do* things too. Not just talk. Like you said, Sam. I wanted to prove it to you both. And to me." She looked at the floor.

Sam smiled. "Marty, you're crazy. Seriously. I mean, okay, you do talk a lot—no, wait, I'm sorry; I didn't mean it that way. It's good, all the talking, all your facts. Who knew about Yorktown and 'Yankee Doodle'? Who knew that Delaware was the first state to sign the Constitution? Who knew how to fix Theo's shoulder? We wouldn't be alive right now if you didn't know all this crazy stuff."

Martina looked up, meeting Sam's gaze, and smiled back, a little weakly.

"He's right," Theo said.

"And I'm sorry I keep calling you Marty," Sam added. "I won't do it anymore."

"No, it's okay," Martina said. "I'm starting to like it now. Nobody's ever given me a nickname before."

Somehow Sam doubted that, but it didn't seem the best time to say it.

"Come on, then," Theo said, and reached down to pull Martina to her feet. "Can you walk?"

"I'm fine," she said. "Now let's get out of here!"

Sam felt confidence sizzling inside him. He liked arguing with Martina, but it was possible that it might be even more fun *not* fighting with her. At least, not all the time.

One after another, Sam, Martina, and Theo walked through the open iron door. "Don't touch the sides!" Martina warned. "It's still connected to the generator." Sam pulled his elbows in close to his ribs, wishing he could make himself skinnier as he eased through.

Beyond the doorway, they found themselves on a small landing before a steep wooden set of stairs leading up into darkness.

"There's no way to shut this door behind us," Theo muttered as he turned back to look at it.

"Flintlock's still locked in the workshop," Sam told him. "Don't sweat it."

"How can you be sure?" Martina asked.

"If he blasted his way through, we'd hear it," Sam said. "But he could use the armonica, like— What's that, Theo?" Sam looked at Theo in surprise as he pulled a folded piece of parchment from his pocket—the sheet music for "Yankee Doodle."

"I grabbed it on the way out," he said.

Sam grinned. "All right, Theo!"

They started up the stairs. It felt good to be heading upward, even if it was into darkness. But after thirty steps—Sam was counting—Martina called out.

"Guess what?"

"A door?" said Sam.

Martina's head lamp showed him he was right. "Well, here goes nothing," she said. She reached for the handle, then grabbed it firmly.

To Sam's surprise, it opened. Martina walked through.

Once he got to the top, Sam paused in astonishment. They were standing on one side of a circular room, perhaps twenty feet across. It looked like something you might find in a big, fancy hotel—shiny wooden door, walls painted white with gold trim. It had a slickly polished wood plank floor, like some kind of nineteenth-century dance hall. It was bright too—lit by natural daylight, if he wasn't mistaken.

And on the other side of the room, there was an open door.

Another *open* door? Could it possibly be that easy? They'd just cross the room and . . . go?

Sam looked around, trying to figure out the trick. Then he looked up.

The ceiling overhead arched into a dome with a round glass window set into its center, and above that there must have been some opening up to the surface, because light from the sun filtered through. Martina was stowing her head lamp away in her backpack.

After spending so much time in dark tunnels lit only by Martina's head lamp, the dim, dusty sunlight felt as good on Sam's face as morning light on the first day of summer vacation.

But by far the strangest thing about the new room was what hung above them. A diamond-shaped metal frame was suspended across the ceiling, just below the window. Filaments of wire were fastened to it like strands of spider's silk. Dozens and dozens of keys hung from the end of these wires, dangling just above their heads. Sam could have easily reached up and touched them.

Big keys and small ones. Iron keys, brass keys, copper keys. Elegant keys that looked more like jewelry than tools to open doors, and plain keys with not a remarkable thing about them.

"Okay," Sam muttered. "Anybody else got a weird feeling about this?"

Martina rubbed the back of her neck as she stared up at the collection of keys. "Definitely."

She lifted a hand toward a golden key with an eagle carved on its handle, so realistic it looked like it was about to soar away on outstretched wings.

"Hey, Marty, don't touch that!" shouted Theo.

She snatched her hand back.

"You've had enough shocks for one day," Theo said. "I think this whole thing is connected to the generator on the other side. See?" Sam's eyes followed a cord draped from the side of the metal frame. It ran down the wall and through the doorway they'd just entered.

He felt it now too—a slight prickle on the back of his neck, as if the air were supercharged.

Martina, a little paler than before, shoved her hands in her pockets. "I should have guessed right away," she said, her head tipped back. "Keys. Benjamin Franklin's kite experiment. That metal diamond is like the kite, and the keys—that's just what he did, hanging a key from a kite. Electricity from the lightning was transferred to the kite, and then to the key. And when Franklin touched the key . . ."

"Ben Franklin's key," Theo said, staring up just like Martina at the maze of keys above his head. "One of these is his. I'm sure of it. And it's what we're here to find. Evangeline called it the Eureka Key. We just have to choose the right one."

"Or we could just . . . go," Sam suggested. "Through that door. The open one. Over there."

"And leave the Eureka Key here? For Flintlock to find? After everything we've been through?" Theo sounded shocked. He didn't look away from the suspended keys.

Why not? Sam wanted to ask. Why shouldn't he walk out, right here, right now, and take Martina with him? Let Theo do whatever he wanted. Why should Sam stay and solve one more deadly puzzle if there was an easy way out?

"Sam," Martina said quietly. "We've come this far. We have to find the answer. Can you really leave a puzzle like this unsolved?"

Theo drew his eyes away from the hanging keys toward Sam. Sam couldn't read the expression on his face. Their gazes met for one heartbeat, then another.

"You lied to us, Theo," Sam told him. "You and Evangeline both did. We don't owe you a thing."

"Go if you want to, Sam," Theo said. "I won't stop you."

Sam looked sideways at Martina. Her eyes were moving back and forth between Sam and Theo; her lower lip caught between her teeth. Sam might not owe Theo anything, but he did owe Martina. She'd risked electrocuting herself to get them through that last door. Was he going to walk out on her?

No.

He'd told his mom that this trip would change him. That it would make him better somehow.

Well, this was his chance.

Sam didn't *have* to do anything for Theo or Evangeline, or even for old Ben Franklin and the Founders. But what if he chose to? If he was willing to use his brain for an Internet puzzle contest or a school prank, wouldn't he do the same to save his country?

"Theo, you better be straight with us from now on," he said. "I mean it."

"You've got it," Theo said with a curt nod.

Sam blinked. He'd expected something more, a bit of an argument, maybe? But Theo, gazing back up at the keys, seemed to think everything was settled.

Sam sighed. For better or for worse, he'd thrown in his hand with these Founders—so he'd better get cracking on this puzzle before it was too late. He began trying to get his head around this final challenge. "Okay. So, we just have to choose the right key? And if we get the wrong one ... zap?"

"Zap," Theo agreed, his mouth set in a straight line.

"How kind of you to explain," said a voice behind them.

Sam whirled around. Flintlock stood at the top of the stairs with a gun in his hand. Sam felt his stomach drop all the way down into his hiking boots.

"It's been quite the game of Follow the Leader," Flintlock said as he walked slowly into the room. Somehow his suit had escaped the worst of the underground ordeal.

The same couldn't be said for the four grumpy-looking men who followed him up the stairs and into the room. They were all wet and looked as if they hadn't enjoyed their day so far at all. But none looked as bad-tempered as the guy with a badly swollen nose. Sam guessed he must have been the one Martina had nailed with her flashlight back on top of the mountain. The thug glared at Martina with the beginning of two black eyes.

Sam frowned. "How'd you get through the workshop door?" he asked. Sam had seen the look in the Flintlock's eyes back up on the mountainside—this man knew about puzzles too. But how had he figured out the trick of the glass armonica without the sheet music and without a walking history textbook like Martina by his side?

"Why, you told us what do to, Mr. Solomon."

"What? Me?"

"You and Miss Wright. A very musical pair. We heard you singing quite clearly." Flintlock's unpleasant smile widened. "And Jed here"—he nodded at the body-builder type next to him, with a frown on his face and a scar that ran from his eyebrow to his jaw—"is actually quite the flautist. He can pick out any tune by ear."

Sam's stomach continued down past his boots, through the floor, and ended up halfway to the Earth's core. One look at Martina's face told him she felt the same.

"Not your fault," Theo told them both.

Flintlock gestured to his men, waving them farther into the room.

"You three—see what's through that door," he told them, and they quickly ran off into the open doorway. "Jed, keep an eye on these kids." Jed, the muscle-bound flautist, moved a little closer to where Sam, Martina, and Theo stood in the center of the room. "Now let me see," Flintlock went on. "What do we have here?" He wandered around the circular room, peering up but keeping an eye—and his gun—on his prisoners as well. "Benjamin Franklin's key. A real piece of history. But which one is it?"

He had stopped beneath the key that Martina had nearly touched earlier. It spun a little in the air, as if the electricity humming inside it made it move. Light glinted off the golden surface.

"An eagle." Flintlock's smile was more of a sneer. "How patriotic. Something tells me *this* is the one. Jed, get it down for me."

"Huh?" Jed looked startled. "Me? I mean . . . sure, Mr. Flintlock." The large man with the scarred face looked up at the keys a little nervously as he crossed the room. He reached up slowly, and Sam glanced over at Martina.

She was frowning. As Sam met her eyes, she shook her head very slightly.

Pop!

Sam was sure he could *hear* electricity leaping from the key to Jed's hand. The instant his huge fist closed around the key, he was flung across the room, so quickly he didn't have time to cry out. He crashed to the floor and lay still.

Rusty metal squealed. The two doors in the walls of the circular room began to slide closed.

Sam grabbed Martina's arm and took two steps toward the way out, only to have a bullet blast into the wooden floor in front of him. They both leaped back, nearly knocking Theo over.

"You're not going anywhere," Flintlock growled.

"But the doors!" Sam said. "We'll be locked in!"

"Yes, we will." Flintlock kept his gun steadily on the three children as the doors clanged shut, the echo ringing in Sam's ears.

"Mr. Flintlock!" On the far side one of the doors, his men were shouting and hammering. "We'll get it open! Just wait!"

"I don't think I'll need to wait long," Flintlock said with confidence. "I think the three of you are going to get that door open for me."

"But we don't know—" Martina started to say.

"Somehow I don't believe that." The gun didn't waver. "You've figured out four of Franklin's puzzles already. Clearly, I didn't have the right idea with that eagle-headed key. Now it's your turn to try."

Theo had moved a small distance away to kneel down by Jed's side. "He's alive," he said, rising back to his feet. "Just unconscious. If you care."

"Not that much." Flintlock shrugged. "Now choose."

Sam looked up at the keys. There must have been fifty of them dangling from above. Maybe more. "Okay, so if this is the key that Franklin used in his experiment," Sam said, thinking out loud, "we can eliminate all the really big keys and really tiny keys. We'll be looking for something relatively average-sized."

"Right," Martina agreed. "But looking at these keys, that still would leave us thirty or so to choose from. We need to eliminate more. Even if we limited the choices to only the silver, copper, and gold keys—which are the best conductors of electricity—that still leaves too many." She shook her head. "It's impossible," Martina said. "How are we supposed to pick the right one?"

"No, it's not impossible. It's a puzzle, just like all the others," Sam said. "It won't be random—so we've got to keep thinking it out."

And the puzzle master here was old Ben Franklin himself. Sam, Theo, Martina, Flintlock—they were all pawns in Ben Franklin's game. To figure out this puzzle then, Sam would have to figure out Ben Franklin. He'd have to think like the Founder.

"Marty," he called out. "Tell us about Ben Franklin."

"Why?" Martina was wandering under the keys, her face turned up, just like Sam and Theo.

"Just do it," he said, echoing Martina's plea in the generator room. "Trust me."

"Okay." Martina started talking. "Um, well—he lived in Philadelphia. He was a printer. He ran away from home when he was seventeen."

"So maybe the seventeenth key?" Sam asked.

"Where would we start counting?" Theo ducked under a low-hanging key. "Which is number one?"

"Yeah, right. That won't work." Sam shook his head. "Keep going, Marty."

"He wrote *Poor Richard's Almanac*," Martina went on. "It had sayings, words to live by. Like 'Never put off till tomorrow what you can do today.' And 'God helps those that help themselves.' And 'Fish and visitors smell in three days.'"

"Seriously? Not if they take a shower. I mean, not the fish. They wouldn't need to . . . never mind. Go on."

"He wasn't born rich, like a lot of the other Founding Fathers—Jefferson, Washington." Martina paused under a giant silver key with stars on its handle that glittered like diamonds and dismissed it. "They had big homes and estates. Not Franklin. He never liked dressing up and showing off. He didn't even buy a wig when he was the ambassador to the French court." Martina's voice was livening up; she sounded almost like she was going to laugh. "He was supposed to wear a powdered wig to court, like all the aristocrats, but he didn't. He just showed up with his bare head, and everybody was shocked. But they loved him for it. All the people in Paris called him 'Le Grand Franklin.'"

Franklin didn't like showing off, Sam thought. *So he wouldn't have a fancy key.* Sam mentally crossed out all the expensive, sparkly keys he saw. But that still left more than a dozen possibilities.

Sam stopped below a simple brass key, about as long as his hand, similar in design to the one that had knocked out Jed. Carved into the handle was another bird with outstretched wings. This bird, however, looked more likely to waddle than to soar.

"Turkey?" he asked in disbelief.

"Do you have to talk about food right now, Sam?" asked Martina. "I'm trying to concentrate—wait. Did you say a turkey?" She hurried over to his side. Sam pointed up to the key he had noticed. "That reminds me of another fun fact," Martina murmured, staring at it. "Franklin thought the turkey should be our national bird instead of the bald eagle." From across the room, Theo stopped and turned, listening. "Turkeys are native to America, see. Eagles aren't. And the eagle is a thief; it steals food from other birds. Turkeys don't. Franklin approved of that. He thought turkeys had courage because they always defended their homes from invaders. But I guess nobody else liked the idea, so we ended up with the eagle."

Despite the locked doors and Flintlock and his gun, Sam had to smile, imagining the dollar bill with a turkey on the back, or the seal of the president with a turkey holding an ear of corn, instead of an eagle with an olive branch. "Well," he muttered, "Franklin and his descendants sure went to a lot of trouble defending this place from invaders, didn't they?"

"So that's it?" Theo said to Martina. "You think that's Franklin's key?"

She nodded. "I think it's our best bet."

"Prove it." Flintlock had been listening intently. Now he stood up straighter, his eyes narrowed. "Go on, girl. Get the key."

Theo took a step forward, but Flintlock held up a hand, ordering him to stay where he was. Martina's eyes moved from the hanging key to Jed's unconscious body.

"No way." Sam put a hand on Martina's shoulder, pushing her back. "I'll do it. I don't know if you'd survive another shock."

Flintlock shrugged. "I really don't care which of you gets it," the man told them. "If you're wrong, I'll still have two more chances to find the right one."

Sam stared at the key. What if old Ben had just put this here as a double bluff? Jed had survived the shock of touching the wrong key, but he was a grown man, a big one. Sam was probably half his size. The electric current that had knocked Jed out might kill Sam with one touch.

"Sam . . . ," Martina whispered, wide-eyed.

"Hey, don't worry, Marty." Sam tried to give her a reassuring grin, but it felt a little shaky around the edges. "But promise me one thing."

Martina bit her lip. "Of course. What is it?"

"If you have to give me mouth-to-mouth—just don't tell me about it when I wake up."

Martina rolled her eyes and chuckled—but it sounded more like a sob.

If I wake up, Sam thought.

He reached for the key.

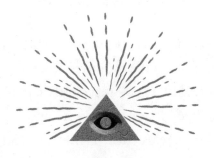

CHAPTER TWELVE

Sam closed his eyes as his trembling fingers made contact with the key. He prepared to feel the jolt of electricity course through his body, prepared for the pain . . .

But the key was cool to the touch.

Sam let out a breath he hadn't realized he was holding and pulled the key toward him. The wire broke with a soft snap.

And just like that, the Eureka Key was in Sam's hand.

"Way to go, Sam." Theo looked more relieved and happy than Sam had ever seen him.

Martina smiled. "I was right," she said, shaking her head. "I can't believe it."

"I can," Sam replied. "I never doubted you." Then he paused. "Much." Martina chuckled.

More important, metal was scraping on stone. Sam turned to see if the door across the room was opening—but it wasn't. It was still firmly shut. Wait—that wasn't fair. He'd picked the right key, hadn't he? Weren't they getting out of here now?

Maybe they were. A slice of the wall to Sam's left slid open. He moved toward it eagerly. Another door?

No. Sam groaned. Not a door. A hole. He peered through the new opening, which led right into another mine shaft, a vertical tunnel running up and down through solid rock, with a ladder heading up one side.

"It must be the real way out," Martina said, peering over Sam's shoulder. "That other door—it was probably a decoy." She glanced quickly at Sam and then away. But Sam didn't have much time to feel embarrassed about how close he'd been to going through the wrong door, because Flintlock's voice rose from behind them.

"Move away from there, both of you. And Mr. Solomon, I'll take that key, thank you very much."

Sam and Martina moved away from the hole. "Okay," Sam told Flintlock. "Here." He took a few steps toward Flintlock, holding the key in his outstretched hand. If Flintlock's attention was on the key, Sam might be able to grab the gun. It could give them all a chance to escape—if he could just pull it off.

But Flintlock seemed to guess what Sam had in mind. "That's close enough," he said, his voice sharp.

"Drop the key right there. You can slide it over here with your foot."

Sam hesitated. As soon as their foe had the key, that was it. Curtains. Flintlock had already shown he'd sacrifice his own goons. What would a bunch of random kids mean to him?

"I said, drop the key right there." Flintlock raised the gun slightly.

"Drop the key? *That* key?" Martina stepped between Sam and Flintlock, right in front of the gun. What was she *doing*? "Don't you know it's a valuable historical artifact? Speaking of history, did you know that Franklin became famous for his writings in electricity? He really knew how to *pull strings* to get his papers in the right hands."

Why is she talking so strangely? thought Sam. *What does she have in mind?* Then Sam saw Martina glance up at the remaining keys above them and make a subtle tugging motion with her hand. She waggled her eyebrows meaningfully. After a moment, Sam got it. *Very clever*, he thought, and nodded back at Martina in understanding.

"Really? I—I didn't know that," Theo stammered from across the room. He'd figured out that Martina was up to something, Sam realized, and was trying to help stall Flintlock.

Sam caught Theo's eye and jerked his head very slightly toward the new exit in the wall of the room. Theo began to edge toward Martina. "Interesting," he went on. "Uh, tell us some more, Marty."

"Do not tell us *anything* more." Flintlock frowned and moved aside, trying to get a clear shot at Sam. Meanwhile, Sam shuffled sideways and Martina moved to block Flintlock's sight, and his aim, once again. "Enough, girl. Do you think this is a game? Should I show you how serious I am?"

She froze. Even her words dried up.

But by now Sam was where he needed to be. He reached up to the wire that had held the Eureka Key, took hold of it, and yanked.

"Run!" he shouted, jumping backward as Theo seized Martina's arm and pulled her aside, out of harm's way, while the diamond frame above them fell and its keys rained down from the ceiling. Lucky for them that Martina's hunch was right—the keys were all interconnected by the wires—and a strong tug on one wire sent them all crashing down, like little electrically charged bombs.

Flintlock lifted both arms to shield himself as the keys scattered around him. Sam turned and ran with the others toward the hole in the wall. The gun went off, cracking in Sam's eardrums, but he didn't look back. He knew it hadn't hit him or either of his friends, and that was all that mattered. Martina was already through, and Theo followed.

Sam lunged forward, grabbed the metal rungs of the ladder, and started climbing. Below Sam, the mine shaft stretched far down into darkness; above him, Theo's feet were moving. *Faster, Theo, faster* . . .

"Virtues!" Martina shouted from above.

"What?" Sam yelled back, and then looked at the metal rung right in front of his nose. A dim light filtered down from somewhere above, enough to let Sam see that the rung had a word engraved on its surface—*Temperance*. The rung above that said *Patience*.

"It's Franklin's thirteen virtues again!" Martina said. "And some of them—"

As he climbed, Sam's right foot landed on the *Patience* rung, and he heard a horrible *crack*. Suddenly nothing was holding his foot anymore; all his weight hung from his sweaty hands.

"—are wrong!" Martina continued from above. "Like *Patience*! Don't step on that one!"

Thanks, Marty . . . Sam's feet scrabbled at the ladder. He found another rung to stand on and his heart started beating again.

Until he heard a voice from below him. "Back down here, boy." Flintlock, about twenty feet below Sam, was leaning into the mine shaft with his gun raised.

"Don't stop!" Sam called up to Theo and Martina. "He won't shoot me!"

"Oh, I will! Happily!" Flintlock's teeth were bared in something that was definitely not a smile.

"Really?" Sam dug the Eureka Key out of his pocket and held it out to one side, dangling it over the abyss. "You shoot me—and I drop this. Are you sure you can get it back?"

Flintlock paused. "I might shoot one of your friends instead," the man countered. "That would make you come down."

"You could, but you might hit me by mistake. Are you sure you want to risk it?" Sam asked.

Sam was trembling with tension, though the hand holding the key out didn't waver. Above him, Martina and Theo were frozen, clinging to the ladder. Sam watched the calculation on Flintlock's face, waiting to see what the man would do.

Flintlock growled in frustration and shoved his gun back in its holster. Clumsily, he scrambled onto the mine shaft ladder.

"Climb, climb!" Sam shouted up to Theo and Martina. He shoved the Eureka Key back into his pocket, and the three kept going upward.

"Mr. Flintlock!" Sam heard a crash from below and another shout. "We got the door down!"

"It's about time," Flintlock snarled. "Get up here!"

Sam's palms were starting to sting from the rough metal rungs, and the muscles in his arms were throbbing. He tried to push aside the feelings, tried to concentrate on the words he could see carved into the ladder.

"Sam, Theo, don't step on—" Martina's voice drifted down.

"Don't say it!" Sam yelled. She'd warn Flintlock and his goons as well as himself and Theo. He had a good memory; he'd just hoped Theo did too. *Chastity.* Safe to step on. *Modesty?* He didn't think so.

"I can see where the light's coming from!" Theo called. "A way out!"

Sam could see it too, a bright circle overhead. *Frugality?* He put his foot on that, and it held his weight. *Moderation?* He wasn't so sure about that. Maybe better to skip it.

A *crack* came from below him. One of the four men below must have stepped on *Modesty,* or maybe *Moderation.* There was a sharp, panicked yell that started loud and got softer and softer . . . until it stopped.

Sam should have been glad. One less person to chase them. One less bad guy to grab the Eureka Key. But he wasn't glad; he was sick, thinking of the sudden drop, and the even more sudden stop.

"Stupid!" he heard Flintlock shout below him. "Follow my lead; step *only* on the rungs I step on. Hurry!"

They climbed and climbed, past some virtues that Sam recognized—there came *Temperance* again, and he already knew to skip *Modesty*—along with some new ones. He passed *Justice* and *Sincerity*, *Order* and *Tranquility*—hah, when was the last time Sam had felt tranquil? Then came *Courage*. Seriously, that one broke under Sam's foot? What did Ben Franklin have against courage?

"Almost there!" Martina called down.

Sam looked up. The circle of light was getting bigger and brighter, and he could see Martina's body outlined against it.

"Theo, get up here with me! I need some help!" she gasped.

Martina inched to one side, giving Theo enough room to climb up on the same rung with her. Sam, still climbing and panting and blinking salty sweat out of his eyes, could see a metal seal, inlaid with a circle of thick glass to let in the light, right above their heads.

Theo put his shoulder against the metal circle and heaved, and the thing swung open. The sunlight that spilled through was hot and bright and dry, and Sam had to squint as he kept climbing, trying to reach his friends in time.

"Sam! Hurry!" Martina shouted.

What did she think he was doing? Strolling? Sam didn't waste breath answering. As his foot came down on *Cleanliness*—who would put *Cleanliness* in a list of virtues and leave off *Courage*?—Theo's hand reached down, closed on Sam's arm, and yanked.

Sam popped out through the hole like a cork out of a bottle, knocking Theo over. The two of them tumbled onto hot, packed dirt. A steep cliff of tawny rock rose over their heads. Martina slammed the metal trapdoor shut behind them.

"Rocks!" she panted. "We need something heavy! Quick!" She was kneeling on the circle of glass and metal, which had been set into a flat patch of dusty rock. The part of Death Valley where they found themselves was scattered with weathered rocks, some the size of a doll's house, others bigger than cars. Theo and Sam scrambled to their feet, and Theo grabbed hold of a rock about the size of a Saint Bernard, putting all his weight behind it. Sam, squinting in the blazing light, did his best to help. Martina ran up and put her shoulder into it as well, and they shoved it onto the circle. When it was done, Sam flopped onto the ground to gasp for breath.

"You still have the key?" Theo asked, leaning on the boulder as he, too, dragged in long, deep breaths.

"Right here." Sam patted the pocket of his jeans. He could still feel the adrenaline pumping through his veins, but he couldn't help grinning up at the blazing blue sky. "We did it. Guys, we did it! We solved every puzzle old Ben Franklin threw at us!"

"Yes. Yes, we did." Martina sat down beside Sam, both of them shaking.

And we didn't do it to play some dumb prank or to show off, Sam thought. *We did it for a good cause. Helping out a friend. Fighting injustice.*

Sam heard his own words to his mom in his mind. *Something important.*

Theo straightened up, looking over the boulder to something along the edge of the cliff. "What's that?"

"What's what?" Sam sat up. "Oh. That." A white van was parked at the base of the cliff, about fifty yards away. "That's . . . kind of weird." He looked around for a road or a parking lot or, even better, a ranger station, or any sign of human life at all. He didn't see a thing . . . except that van. "How'd that get here?"

"I drove it, naturally," said a smooth voice behind them.

Sam jerked to his feet as if the Eureka Key *had* given him an electric shock this time. A man in an immaculate white suit stepped out from behind a boulder. He pulled off a pair of sunglasses, showing a smooth face that looked young, despite the white hair that was combed back from his forehead. Light-blue eyes, narrowed a little against the glare of the sun, studied the three children with a cool curiosity, as if they were scientific specimens he was planning to dissect. The man's pale skin, coupled with his white suit, made him look like some kind of angel in the middle of the desert. Could he be there to rescue them from all this?

Sam heard Theo suck in a sharp breath. "Arnold," he said softly. And for the first time since Sam had met him, Theo looked afraid.

Sam's heart plummeted. Not an angel after all.

But the man didn't seem interested in Theo at all; his attention was on Sam.

"I believe, young man," he said, "that you have something that belongs to me."

CHAPTER THIRTEEN

The van shook and bounced as it rattled its way across the desert. Sam, sitting on the floor in the back, braced himself, trying to keep from toppling over onto Theo, on one side of him, or Martina, on the other.

The windows had been painted over, so the only light came from the cracks around the doors. It was hot too. At least the dark windows kept out the blazing sun, but Sam longed for the air-conditioning that there must be up front. Surely that guy named Arnold was driving along in comfort while the three kids sweated and sweltered in the back.

Arnold had forced Sam, Theo, and Martina to let Flint-lock and his two remaining men out of the mine shaft. Nobody had been concerned about the man who'd been electrocuted, and when Martina had tried to tell Arnold that the poor guy was still down there, he'd turned a look of such cold indifference on her that she'd stuttered into silence.

Then Arnold had ordered the three kids into the van and shut the door on them. There was no handle or release on this side of the door; Theo had checked immediately. No way out.

Sam sat lost in gloomy thought as the van lurched over the uneven ground. He'd thought they had made it, he really had. After all the puzzles and the fear and the craziness and the fact that he—Sam Solomon, the kid with the Rubik's Cube—had suddenly become sort of responsible for saving the country and maybe the world, he'd been feeling good. Like maybe all those teachers and principals and parents talking about his potential had been right after all.

And then this guy Arnold, who was frankly scarier than Flintlock (and Sam hadn't thought that was possible) had shown up. And everything they'd done had been taken away from them. Just like that.

The look that flashed across Theo's face when Arnold had stepped from behind that rock was what really spooked Sam. Theo hadn't acted scared all day long. Not when his shoulder had been out of joint. Not when the ceiling had been coming down on his head. But Arnold—that guy scared *Theo*.

"What time is it?" Sam asked.

"Why does it matter?" Martina sounded just as gloomy as Sam felt.

"I don't know. I'm just hungry." Sam thought back to the banana and cinnamon roll he'd snagged from the breakfast buffet at the hotel, so many hours ago. Back when life was normal. Back when he hadn't known about the Founders or Ben Franklin's key. "Wish we still had our backpacks." Arnold and Flintlock had confiscated the packs when they'd ordered the three kids into the back of the van. "I think I left a Snickers bar in there somewhere."

Nobody answered.

"So, Theo." Sam figured it was up to him to talk, since nobody else seemed interested. "Who is that guy? Arnold? You seemed to know him."

"I know him." Theo stared straight ahead, apparently lost in thought—and not pleasant thought either.

"Come on, man. Talk to us." Sam nudged him with an elbow. "We've got to figure out what to do next."

Theo shook his head and rubbed both hands over his face. "What to do next. Right."

Sam waited. After a minute of silence he said, "Well?"

Theo sighed and lifted his face out of his hands. "His name's Gideon Arnold. He's the one who killed Evangeline's father. And"—Sam could have sworn he heard Theo's voice crack—"maybe some other people too."

Sam felt the blood drain from his face.

"His last name is Arnold, not his first name?" Martina asked.

"Yes," Theo answered, sounding miserable.

"He wouldn't happen to be related to a certain famous person from the Revolution too, would he?"

"Yeah. He is."

Sam looked back and forth between Theo and Martina, not quite understanding what she was getting at. "Related? To whom?"

Theo stared at him. "Benedict Arnold."

"Whoa, really?" Sam frowned. "I know he was kind of a bad guy, but—"

"*Kind of?*" Theo seemed to come back to life, his voice growing louder with anger. "There wasn't any 'kind of' about it. Benedict Arnold started out as an officer in George Washington's army—"

"Some people even called him a hero," Martina chimed in. "I mean, he really did have a brilliant mind for strategy, but—"

"He wasn't any kind of hero," Theo said, cutting her off. Sam was shocked. This was by far the most emotion he'd seen from Theo since they met. "Arnold didn't get the promotion he thought he deserved, so he got in touch with the British. He was going to hand West Point—and George Washington himself—over to them, if they paid him enough. He planned to sell out the people who trusted him the most."

"Wow," Sam said. "That's pretty harsh, just because he didn't get a shiny medal or whatever."

Theo nodded. "But when his British contact was captured, Arnold ran and left him to be hanged. So in the end, he was a traitor to both sides of the Revolution."

"Great." Sam pulled up his T-shirt to wipe the sweat from his face. "And we've got a member of the charming Arnold family driving this van? Wonderful."

"If Gideon is a descendant of Benedict Arnold," Martina said thoughtfully, "and Evangeline is a descendant of Benjamin Franklin—who are you a descendant of, Theo?"

Theo looked over at her, startled.

"You told us you were one of them. One of the Founders. But you never told us which one."

Theo hesitated for a second or two. Then he rolled up his sleeve and leaned forward a little so his left arm was in the light. On the inside of his forearm, Sam could see a small black tattoo. An eye, unblinking, hovered over a pyramid, and inside the pyramid there was a sword.

"The sword stands for courage," Theo said. "It's the symbol of the Washington family."

"Wow." Martina drew in a breath. "George Washington? Really?"

Theo nodded and rolled his sleeve back down. "I'm his great-great-great-great-great-great-great-grandnephew. I think. Maybe one more great."

"Wow," Martina repeated. "If we get out of this alive, I want your autograph."

Theo grunted. "It's not . . . like that. I mean, it's something to live up to, but . . . look at me. My first real mission, and I already failed. The Eureka Key is in the enemy's hands, and so are we."

The van shifted, and its tires ground briefly in gravel. Sam could feel that they were now headed up a hill. "You can't give up yet, man," Sam said. "Even George Washington lost a battle now and then, but he didn't lose the war."

"Sam's right," Martina added.

Before Theo could answer them, the van lurched to a halt and Sam and Martina tumbled into a heap. A second later, the doors were flung open.

Tall figures were standing outside, black silhouettes against the light, and strong hands reached in to haul the three kids out. The sunlight wasn't as bright as it had been; it was taking on a golden tone that hinted of early evening. But after the dark van, it was still enough to dazzle Sam's eyes.

Once he could see again, Sam saw that Flintlock had taken hold of Theo, and one of his men had a hand around Martina's arm and the other on the collar of Sam's shirt.

Gideon Arnold was nearby, and all of them were standing in front of . . . a castle?

How did *that* get here?

It looked like something from a movie set—cream-colored walls, red roofs, arched doorways, and flags fluttering from turrets. "Welcome to Scotty's Castle," Gideon Arnold said. "My home away from home."

"Nice place," Sam said weakly. "Got Wi-Fi?"

Nobody laughed, but maybe that was because two all-terrain vehicles were roaring up, each carrying a pair of men. When they got off, Sam saw how big they were. And how grim their faces looked. It was as if Arnold and Flintlock had a thug factory somewhere that just kept popping out new goons.

"It's part of the park," Martina said, her words coming out quickly. She was back in her encyclopedia mode; Sam recognized it. And now he realized that a rush of facts was how Martina coped with nervousness, or outright terror. "I read about it," she went on. "There was this cowboy and prospector, Death Valley Scotty, who had it built. He said it was with the money from his secret gold mine. He was a big liar, though, so nobody actually believed him, but . . . um, where did all the tourists go?"

"The castle closes at four thirty, and I have paid handsomely to have the place to myself after-hours," Gideon

Arnold answered, eyeing her closely. "I've heard about your extraordinary grasp of history, Miss Wright. It's quite impressive."

Martina got quiet.

"There's no one around for miles, so I wouldn't advise trying to escape," Arnold went on. "You wouldn't get far in the desert. Shall we go in?"

"Maybe another time, thanks all the same," Sam muttered.

Arnold laughed. "I know all about you too, Mr. Solomon, and your smart mouth. Follow me."

With Flintlock still holding onto Theo, and with his man keeping a tight grip on Sam and Martina, they didn't have much choice. They followed Arnold through the castle gates.

It looked like a nice enough place, if there weren't big, ugly, armed men pushing you into it. The three kids were herded down a hallway and into a two-story room. There, Flintlock let Theo go with a shove, and the man holding Sam and Martina released them as well. Sam took a look around.

A heavy iron chandelier hung overhead. Couches and chairs, all shiny wood and soft cushions, beckoned, reminding Sam how tired he was. Wood was piled in a big fireplace, ready for a match once the desert night turned cold.

Arnold settled into a fancy wingback armchair as if it were a throne. "So the Founders have been reduced to sending children on their missions," he said thoughtfully. "My goodness, how the mighty have fallen." He shook his head and smiled indulgently at Theo's furious glare. Then he nodded at Flintlock, who advanced on Sam.

Sam took a step back and bumped into somebody who took hold of both his arms.

"If we all stay calm, this will be over fairly quickly," Arnold said, taking a silver revolver out of a holster inside his suit jacket and leveling it at Theo, who looked ready to leap to Sam's defense. "My men have searched all your packs, and found no trace of the key. I'm a reasonable man, children. Just hand it over."

With an eye on the dangerous-looking men surrounding them, Sam decided that he'd have to comply, if only to buy them some time to figure out a plan. He twisted free from the man behind him, who let him go. Reluctantly, Sam pulled the key from his pocket and held it out in his hand. Flintlock snatched it from his outstretched palm and handed it to Arnold. The man's eyes locked on to the key, and he turned it slowly in the light. "Such a plain little thing," he mused after a moment. "Amazing that so much power will come from wielding it."

"You have no right to take it," Martina spoke up. "You're not part of the Franklin family. If it belongs to anyone, it's Evangeline."

"He doesn't care." Theo's voice was scornful. "He's a thief and a traitor. Just like his ancestor."

Arnold stood, straightening his jacket, and walked over to Theo. The way he looked at Theo could have blistered paint on the wall. Sam felt a shiver work its way up his spine.

"Benedict Arnold tried to sell out the people who trusted him," Theo said, meeting Arnold's glare with one of his own and holding his chin up high. "He didn't know what loyalty was. Or honor."

"You know your history as well, I see," Arnold said. "Your version of it, at least."

Then he slapped Theo across the face. Sam jumped; Martina gasped. Theo stood as solidly as a deeply rooted tree and didn't make a sound.

"Is that what you've been taught, Mr. Washington?" Arnold asked. "History sometimes forgets the truth, you know. Benedict Arnold was a military genius. Your illustrious ancestor would not have gotten as far as he did without *my* ancestor's help. He was wounded and crippled, fighting for a desperate cause, and then cast aside by the commander he served. Small-minded men attacked and accused him, and in their jealousy they drove him to do what he did. Today no one remembers his triumphs and his victories. But that is something I plan to change, once I get my hands on the Founders' weapon."

"I don't know what you're talking about," said Theo.

"Nice try, Mr. Washington," said Arnold. "You Founders all pride yourselves on your secrets, but I know everything, thanks to Victor Temple. Evangeline's papa was quite a talker, when we got him into the right . . . frame of mind."

"You tortured him, you animal!" Theo snarled.

Arnold leaned even closer to Theo. "I used my powers of persuasion, that's all." He turned and walked away, leaving Theo seething with fury. "My first instinct was just to kill you all—no one would have suspected anything if that tiny plane had crashed in the desert. But somehow you survived, and being from a family of great strategic vision, I changed tack to accommodate. I realized I could use you instead. Why bother searching for the key ourselves, when you could just lead us straight to it?" He paused and looked at Sam. "I didn't think you'd make it quite so easy."

Arnold held the key up to the light and turned it slowly, studying every inch, from the turkey carved on the handle to the long, elegant shaft. "In his final hours, Victor Temple told me that the Eureka Key would reveal where to search for the next artifact."

Sam stood frozen, staring at Arnold and the key. Once Arnold had found the clue—what next? He wouldn't need Theo or Martina or Sam himself any longer, would he? And Sam was getting a very bad feeling about what happened to people whom Gideon Arnold no longer needed.

Arnold was frowning at the key with distaste. "Benjamin Franklin enjoyed his childish little puzzles," he muttered, and then he looked up, his gaze landing on Sam. "How appropriate that we have children here, then. Let me see for myself what Evangeline Temple saw in you, Mr. Solomon," he said, and tossed the key through the air.

Automatically, Sam put up his hands to catch it. "Why should I help you?" he asked.

Arnold smiled at him with a touch of pity. "You don't actually need me to answer that, do you?"

The man Martina had hit with her flashlight was standing close behind her. At Arnold's words, he grabbed hold of her arm, clamping his other hand over her mouth and nose. He grinned as she made a startled, choking sound.

"Stop it! Let her go!" Sam cried out.

"Of course, Mr. Solomon. As soon as you tell me what that key has to say."

Sam looked at Martina's face, her glasses askew, her eyes wide over the hand that was stifling her, and quickly turned his attention to the key.

"You're happy to sacrifice innocent people to get what you want," Theo said to Arnold, his fists clenched. "I see the apple doesn't fall far from the tree."

Gideon Arnold shrugged. "How many of George Washington's soldiers died in battle? Great leaders do what is necessary to win. If you had a real drop of *your* ancestor's blood flowing through your veins, you would know that."

Theo winced, looking more injured by Gideon's words than by his slap.

Sam tuned them both out, his attention on the key in his hand. How was he supposed to solve another puzzle without Martina's help? It was Martina who knew all about American history. Her brain full of facts had led them to Franklin's key. Now she was struggling breathlessly, depending on *him*.

Sam's heart began to pick up the pace, and his breath was coming more quickly. Was there something hidden in the carving of the turkey? Letters or numbers somewhere among the feathers of its wings? He couldn't see anything like that. And Martina was twisting in the thug's grasp, trying to pull her head away from the hand over her face.

"We don't have all day," Gideon Arnold said calmly. "At least, Miss Wright doesn't. I'd say another minute at best."

Sam would have loved to shoot Arnold the nastiest look he could manage, but he didn't dare spare the time. He kept his eyes on the key. He couldn't see any clue. But he could *feel* something. The key felt light in his hand, lighter than it should. Maybe that was because it was . . . hollow?

He took the handle in one hand and the shaft of the key in the other, and he twisted.

The metal resisted for a moment, and then gave way. As quickly as he could, he unscrewed the shaft from the handle, turned it upside down, and shook it. A tiny, rolled-up parchment, light as a feather, drifted into his upturned palm.

"Okay!" he said. "I got it! Let her go!"

Arnold nodded. The man holding Martina released his grip, and she stumbled away from him, falling onto her knees and gasping.

Sam moved to her side, steadying her with a hand on her shoulder. "Here," he said. "You look, Marty." He figured she deserved it.

But Arnold crossed the room in a few steps and held out a hand, snapping his fingers. "I'll take that."

Reluctantly, Sam put the scrap of parchment into his hand. A smile lifted one corner of Arnold's mouth as he carefully unrolled it.

Then the smile vanished.

"More games." He looked back up. "Miss Wright, perhaps it's your turn. Do you need some . . . . persuasion, like Mr. Solomon? Or can you simply tell me what this means?"

Martina held out her hand, her eyes narrowed.

Arnold shook his head. "I don't think so. You might think of destroying it. Just look."

He held the paper out so Martina could see it. Sam looked over her shoulder.

It was a drawing. A mountain. Some kind of animal with curvy horns underneath it. To the left, a foot, colored black with heavy ink. To the right, a strange-looking person with a head sheared off at the top, like he'd been given a flattop that went horribly wrong.

Martina rubbed her hands over her face one last time and shook her head. "I—I don't know . . ."

Sam shrugged. "Maybe it's Ben Franklin's idea of a joke."

The back of Arnold's hand smacked into the side of his face.

Sam staggered and fell, bouncing off an armchair on the way down. He heard the Eureka Key hit the ground and tried to stand.

"Sam!" Martina arrived at his side as Theo bent and picked the key up.

"Hand it over," Flintlock growled. Theo did so without a word.

"Are you okay?" Martina asked, helping Sam sit up.

"Uh. I think so," Sam muttered, rubbing his cheek. He could taste blood inside his mouth, but he was pretty sure all his teeth were still attached.

Martina touched Sam's arm lightly. She glanced at the door twenty feet away, and Sam knew that she was thinking exactly what he was thinking. Gideon and Flintlock were staring at the scrap of parchment. Their men all had their eyes on the bosses, waiting for the next order. Then Martina reached down to a pocket on her hiking pants and silently pulled the zipper open. She slipped something out—it looked like a stick of dynamite, or a hot dog. No ... it was a flare.

A horrible thought struck Sam. *Waterproof?* he mouthed. What if getting soaked in that flooded mine shaft had ruined the flare? What if it wouldn't even burn?

Martina nodded just a little bit. "You know me," she murmured. "Always prepared."

Trust Martina not to venture out in the desert without a waterproof distress flare to catch the attention of rescue planes in case she got lost.

Sam caught Theo's eye, and then flicked his gaze toward the door. Theo frowned. There was no way Sam could clue him in to Martina's plan; he just had to trust Theo to be ready to move as soon as the flare went off.

Sam stood up, pretending to lean on Martina's arm, but actually shielding her from the sight of Gideon Arnold and his men. Slowly and quietly, she slipped the cap off the end of the flare.

Gripping the cap in her left hand and the flare in her right, Martina drew her right hand back.

"Nonsense. It's utter nonsense," Arnold muttered. "You two . . ." He scowled and looked up, and his eyes went wide.

"Surprise!" Martina shouted. She smashed the end of the flare against the cap and threw it straight at Arnold.

Suddenly the room was blazing with light. It hurt Sam's eyes, even though he kept his hand over them as he scrambled to his feet and threw himself in the direction where he thought the door must be.

"Fire! Fire!" somebody was yelling.

Martina was beside Sam. "Go!" Theo shouted from behind.

But the key—they were leaving the Eureka Key behind in the hands of the enemy!

There was nothing Sam could do about that. The only thing they could do now was run. Sam thumped into the door of the room, knocking it open, and the three kids plowed out into the hallway and then outside.

The sun had set, although the glow from below the horizon still lit up a deep-blue sky. Sam hesitated for a moment, unsure which way to go. Where could they hide?

Then he heard Martina yell from next to one of the ATVs. "Over here! The keys are still in this one!"

"Can you drive that?" Sam asked, sprinting to her side. The ATV had four thick, black wheels and two seats, for a driver and a single passenger.

"Probably better than you!" Martina told Sam.

"Hey, you're talking to a top scorer on *Need for Speed*," Sam retorted.

"Really." Martina crossed her arms. "A video game. And you think that makes you an expert?"

"No arguing now. *I'm* driving!" Theo snapped. "You two get in the back!"

They did. Sam and Martina squashed into the passenger seat behind Theo as he twisted the key in the ignition. The engine sputtered then roared into life, and Sam and Martina were nearly thrown off as Theo kicked the machine into gear and sped downhill, heading along the driveway and away from the castle.

They hadn't gone far before Theo threw his weight against the handlebars and turned the bike off-road onto the hard-packed dirt. The headlights bounced crazily, lighting up scrubby brush and ragged foothills. Sam's stomach bounced too, up into his throat and back down again as the machine barreled over a rise in the ground, kicking up clouds of grit and dust, and then crashed through a bush and startled a dozing jackrabbit, who ran for its life.

After dropping heavily into a dry creek bed, Theo turned again to follow the creek's course. They skidded around a few curves, and then Theo yanked the vehicle to a stop and switched off the engine. A small hill rose over them, cutting them off from the sight of anyone near the castle.

"Quiet!" he whispered. "Listen!"

Sam's ears were still echoing with the rumble of the engine and the pounding of his own heart. Then he heard a sound that made his heart sink—more engines roaring to life. The other ATVs back at the castle? The white van?

"Maybe they didn't see which way we went," Martina whispered. "It's dark out—that could cover our tracks." Theo waved a hand to quiet her. All three of them crouched low on the ATV's seats, listening.

The engines were getting louder. Sam tensed. Should they take off now? Should they stay still, hoping Arnold and his men would overlook them?

He saw Theo's hand move to the ATV key. The growl of the nearest engine grew louder, and then light shone over the top of the hill that was their cover. An ATV had topped the rise over their heads, and caught them in the beams of its headlights.

"Go!" yelled Sam.

Theo twisted the key hard, and their own engine roared back to life just as a gun went off and a rock close by Sam's foot exploded into shards. This time there would be no second chances, he realized. If they got caught, they were dead.

The other ATV bounced down the slope toward them, and Sam hung on hard to Martina as Theo raced the machine down the path of the creek bed. Then the ground softened beneath them and their ATV tipped, two wheels spinning helplessly in the air.

Sam threw his weight sideways, trying to steady the ATV, and Martina did the same. Another bullet plowed into the earth to their right. But they got all the wheels on the ground, and Theo drove out of the creek bed, tearing up a small hill and crashing down onto flatter land beyond.

The other ATV struggled up the hill behind them, and a second was close on its tail. To his right, Sam saw Scotty's Castle again, outlined against the darkening sky. The white van was careening down a hill from the castle's parking lot, headed straight toward them.

"We can't outrun them!" Theo shouted as he drove.

Sam knew he was right. If they went straight, they'd be shot. If they wove back and forth across the landscape, they'd be a more difficult target to hit, but they'd lose speed.

"Just keep going!" he yelled.

Theo twisted the handlebars, aiming the ATV at a gap between two low hills perhaps fifty yards away. A third bullet whined through the air above them; Sam ducked, pushing Martina down too. They both clung on, lurching from side to side as the ATV raced across the desert.

The hills were getting closer. Maybe they'd make it to the gap. That could get them out of their pursuers' sight for a minute or two. And then what?

Suddenly a fierce white light blazed into his face.

Headlights! Another vehicle had barreled out of the gap between the hills, right into their path.

Theo tried to turn, but he was going too fast. The ATV skidded across packed dirt. Martina cried out. Sam tightened all his muscles, bracing for impact.

Chapter Fourteen

The ATV tipped again, rising up on its two right wheels. Blinded by light and dust, breathing in clouds of choking grit, Sam lost his grip on Martina and went tumbling across the dirt, crashing into a thorny bush.

For a few panicked seconds, he couldn't breathe or move. Then, slowly, the vise-grip across his chest loosened and he managed to cough. He peeled his eyes open, unable to see anything but brightness. Was this the shining light everybody always talked about in the afterlife? Was he about to hear a deep voice welcoming him to eternity, and perhaps mentioning that time he'd stolen the tadpoles from the science lab and dumped them into the water cooler in the teachers' lounge?

No, he was actually blinking in the glare of headlights that belonged to a massive SUV, screeching to a stop not three feet from where Sam was lying.

Someone was shouting, "It's them!" Doors were banging open; people were jumping out of the vehicle. Sam groaned. He was dusty, tired, and bruised, and he didn't think he could run away from anybody anymore.

"Theodore?" A tall, slender figure was striding through the light-flare.

"It's us, Evangeline," Theo called. "Sam? Marty? You okay?"

Theo had picked himself up and was walking toward the woman who Sam now recognized as Evangeline. She wore a rumpled tan coat, and wisps of steel-gray hair had escaped from her bun. She looked older somehow, as if the past twelve hours had aged her twelve years. When her eyes met Sam's, he saw her thin shoulders sink with relief.

Martina was on her hands and knees, groping around for her glasses. Sam kicked and crawled his way out of the bush, ignoring the stinging scratches. Evangeline had about half a dozen people with her, who were all wearing park ranger uniforms.

Saved, Sam thought. *And not a moment too soon.*

Gideon Arnold's white van was still coming toward them, now about fifty yards away. The two ATVs were hanging back, perhaps waiting to see what happened next, but as Sam watched, the van approached and braked, bouncing a little on its wheels, and Flintlock and Arnold both stepped out.

Park rangers didn't carry guns, did they? Sam felt his stomach do a quick, queasy roll. What if Arnold decided that he wanted the kids back, and didn't care how many witnesses he had to . . . remove? This was the man who'd tortured Evangeline's father to death, after all. Presumably a few park rangers wouldn't mean all that much to him.

But Arnold paused and smoothed his hair with one hand. Sam could see his mind working as his eyes roamed over the scene: Evangeline, talking urgently to Theo; Sam and Martina on the ground; park rangers taking in the scene.

Evangeline stepped out in front of Theo, like a lioness protecting her cub, and faced Gideon Arnold.

Sam could almost hear the hatred sizzling between them. "Well, finally," Arnold said as he straightened his suit jacket with a tug and advanced toward them. "I'm so glad to see an authority figure has arrived. These kids—we saw them on the road, and of course we knew they had no business out alone at night. We tried to flag them down, but they just took off across the desert. I was terribly worried they'd get lost or hurt. Very reckless behavior. I trust you'll speak to their parents? Or their"—his eyes rested on Evangeline—"guardian?"

Sam, his throat full of dust, nearly choked on the hugeness of Gideon's lies. "Hey!" he spluttered. He staggered to his feet. Martina did too. "That's not—"

"I am their guardian," Evangeline said coldly. "I'll certainly be speaking to them about their . . . behavior."

"Wait a second!" Sam protested again. But before he could continue, Theo made a face at him and shook his head.

"You are very kind to be so concerned. I will take responsibility from here." Each word of Evangeline's was edged as sharply as a razor. The rangers looked from one to the other, baffled by the tension that seemed about to make the dry desert air burst into flames.

"Very good, madam," Arnold said. "Well, we should be on our way then."

"Yes," Evangeline hissed. "You should."

Arnold jerked his head at Flintlock and they quickly returned to the white van. The engine started up, and they were gone in a matter of seconds, followed closely by the men on the ATVs.

Sam stumbled to Evangeline's side. "You're letting him go?" he asked under his breath. "But we could—"

"—have him arrested!" Martina finished for him. "Kidnapping. Assault. He hit Sam! And Theo! He was going to shoot us!"

"Would you mind explaining what's going on here?" said one of the rangers. Theo gave his head a quick jerk, warning them both to keep silent. It wasn't easy, but Sam swallowed his protests.

"It's nothing," said Theo. "We just got bored with the sightseeing tour and took off on our own. Couldn't find our way back and got lost."

The head ranger looked skeptical and annoyed. "Do you kids have any idea how lucky you are?" he said. "The next time you decide to wander off from a guided tour, think twice, okay?"

"We're sorry, sir," Theo said. "It won't happen again."

Sam grumbled under his breath. "Lucky" wasn't exactly the term he'd have used.

The rangers handed out water bottles, examined bruises, bandaged scrapes—Sam had not even realized how many spots were bleeding—and one gave Sam an ice pack for his aching cheek.

"How did you find us?" Martina asked Evangeline while one of the rangers was checking out Theo's shoulder.

Evangeline nodded at Theo, a few feet away, who was pulling his T-shirt back over his head. Sam glimpsed a tiny black square on his chest before the T-shirt hid it from view.

"Theodore has a satellite beacon, for emergencies. I've been monitoring it constantly since the three of you disappeared on that canyon tour. For a long time there was no signal at all, which was worrisome."

"We were underground," Martina explained. "All that rock would have blocked the signal."

"I see." Evangeline looked wary, throwing a sideways glance toward the rangers nearby. "In any case, I kept an eye on the satellite signal, and not long ago, it came back online, showing a location near Scotty's Castle. I gathered reinforcements and got here as quickly as I could."

Martina shivered. "I don't know what we would have done if you hadn't."

Evangeline gave her a considering look and then a surprisingly warm smile. "I don't know either, Miss Wright. But I expect you would have done something."

Martina blushed a little.

"At any rate," Evangeline continued, "I look forward to hearing more about your . . . adventures."

"Ms. Temple?" one of the rangers called. "We'd better be heading back."

"Yes, of course," Evangeline agreed. The rangers moved out of earshot as they packed all the first-aid gear back in the SUV.

"Did you get it?" Evangeline whispered as Theo reached her side.

Sam knew what she meant. The Eureka Key—the one that was in Gideon Arnold's pocket right now.

He drew a breath, ready to answer her, when the look on Theo's face stopped him. Old stone-faced Theo was smiling. But why?

Theo put a hand into the pocket of his jeans and pulled out—a key?

"But you gave it to Arnold!" Sam said. "I saw you!"

"You saw me give him *a* key," Theo said. "But not this one. Remember the key with the eagle on its handle? I grabbed it, down in the vault. When I went to check on the guy who got electrocuted, the eagle key was lying there on the floor, right beside him. After Arnold hit you—which was an excellent diversion, thank you, Sam—I switched the keys."

"You're so welcome," Sam muttered, rubbing his sore face.

"I handed Arnold the fake key and slipped the real one into my pocket," Theo went on. "He didn't know what it was supposed to look like—only Flintlock did."

"I can't believe you got away with that," Sam said, shaking his head. "Man, Theo, looks like you didn't need to win a contest to prove you're a genius." Theo blushed and gave Sam a playful punch in the arm.

Evangeline was deaf to their banter. She reached out a trembling hand, and Theo gently laid the key in her palm.

"I never thought I'd hold this," she murmured reverently. "Well done." She closed her fingers around the key and stowed it away inside her purse.

"I couldn't have done it without these two," Theo said. "They know about the Founders, Evangeline. I had to tell them."

Evangeline nodded. "How much do they know?"

Sam spoke up. "Not nearly enough. It took him a while even just to tell us that we weren't actually on a sightseeing trip." He thought Evangeline looked a little bit guilty. "And maybe somebody wants to let me in on why we just let that Arnold guy drive off into the desert?"

"Gideon Arnold has friends in very high places," Evangeline told him. "He wouldn't spend long in jail, I assure you. And questions from the police would mean publicity for things *we must keep secret*." Her eyes met Sam's. Sam had to fight the urge to take a step backward. Evangeline could look scary when she wanted to.

"Don't worry, Mr. Solomon," Evangeline went on, as the rangers beckoned them toward the SUV. "We'll deal with Gideon Arnold on our own terms. But we *will* deal with him. I promise you that."

Morning light touched Sam's face gently. Opening his eyes, he was relieved to see the white walls of his hotel room around him. He rolled over, trying to burrow back into the pillow, but the movement woke a hundred tiny but insistent pains in his back, shoulders, and legs. Muscles that had done more climbing, swimming, falling, running, and scrambling yesterday than Sam had ever done in his life were shouting at him.

Sam gave up. He wasn't going to be able to go back to sleep. Heaving himself upright, he looked down and realized he was still wearing yesterday's clothes, caked with dirt and dust and a fair bit of blood. Yuck. He stripped them off and stumbled into the shower, letting hot water wash away the dirt and the worst of the aches.

When he stepped out of the shower, he wiped the mirror clean and took a look at his face. His cheek, where Arnold had hit him, had darkened to a remarkable shade of purple. There were scrapes on both elbows and another eye-catching bruise across his left shoulder—had that happened when he'd fallen off the ATV? Or when they'd fallen down the mine shaft? And the bush he'd landed in had scribbled scratches across his face and hands as well.

Under all the injuries, though, did his face itself look different? Sam squinted into the mirror, trying to figure it out.

Was he still the Sam who'd nearly missed a plane in Las Vegas? The one who'd begged his mom to let him go on this trip, promising that it would change him? Or was he the Sam who'd faced down bad guys, found a secret key, and discovered more about the history of his country than he'd ever imagined?

Too complicated a question to ask on an empty stomach. There had been some food last night, he thought, after a ride back to the Furnace Creek Ranch that he only hazily remembered. But apparently it hadn't been enough. He could consider deep philosophical questions after he'd eaten some bacon.

Probably a lot of bacon.

He pulled on clean jeans and a T-shirt and headed for the door, looking down when he heard a slight crunch beneath his foot. He'd stepped on a piece of paper. Picking it up, he saw that there was a message written on it in swirly handwriting: *Meet me on the portico.*

Sam detoured by the breakfast buffet first.

When he reached the covered entranceway to the ranch's main building, he saw Evangeline sitting in a rocking chair, sipping a cup of coffee, with Theo by her side.

Theo, wearing a white button-down shirt over his jeans, looked all serious again, just as he had when Sam had first met him. Evangeline was gazing out over the view. She wore a sleeveless dress with a wrap over her shoulders. On her left arm, the wrap had slipped down, and Sam could see a tattoo, standing out clearly against her fair skin. It was exactly like Theo's, except for one thing—inside the one-eyed pyramid, where Theo's tattoo had a sword, Evangeline's tattoo had a key.

Evangeline didn't seem to notice that Sam had arrived. Sam, munching on a breakfast burrito, looked out over the landscape to see if he could spot what she was looking at.

The early morning light was spilling down the slopes of pale-brown mountains, and stretching over miles and miles of hills, tawny with dry grass and brush. Little clouds, pale pink and soft orange, floated in a sky bluer than any Sam had ever seen.

On the lawn, an American flag flapped gently in the soft breeze. "'Oh, say, can you see,'" Evangeline murmured tunefully, almost to herself, "'by the dawn's early light, what so proudly we hailed, at the twilight's last gleaming?'"

If there was going to be singing, Sam hoped he could get away with standing in the back row and moving his lips.

"Do you know what that song refers to, Mr. Solomon?"

Sam stopped mid-chew. So Evangeline *did* notice his arrival. "Um, no," he said through a mouthful. He'd never really thought about it. It was just the national anthem, just something to get through as quickly as possible so the baseball game could start.

"The British attack on Fort McHenry." Now Evangeline did turn her head to look at Sam. "In Baltimore, during the War of 1812. The British shelled the fort all night long. But when the sun rose in the morning, the Stars and Stripes was still flying. The Americans had won."

"Oh." Sam swallowed.

"It amazed many at the time," Evangeline continued. "How a force that seemed so weak at first could prevail against such overpowering strength. But you know all about that, don't you, Mr. Solomon?"

To his intense embarrassment, Sam felt himself blushing.

"You did very well yesterday. You and Miss Wright. Theodore filled me in on the details." Evangeline's expression turned serious. "You were angry at him, and at me as well. But I hope you can understand why we needed to be sure we could trust you. These secrets . . . no one outside the Founders has ever been entrusted with them before."

Sam felt the heat in his cheeks draining away. "I don't like being kept in the dark," he answered her.

"Of course. But you've met Gideon Arnold now, so you must understand why we needed to keep silent," Evangeline went on. "After what happened with the plane, I was almost sure you were on our side. But I wanted to be absolutely certain before I told you the truth. I had no idea that Arnold and his followers would move so quickly. Still, I owe you an apology."

Sam didn't know what to say. He'd done plenty of apologizing to adults in his time, but he thought this might be the first time an adult had actually apologized to him. "It's okay," he said. "I mean, not exactly okay. But, um, I understand. And I accept your apology."

Now Theo really was smiling. And Evangeline too. It was surprising what a difference it made on her thin, severe face.

"Did I miss anything?" It was Martina's voice. She had arrived on the portico as well, with another of Evangeline's notes in her hand.

"I was telling Mr. Solomon how impressed I was with your performance yesterday. When courage and cleverness come together, there is little they can't accomplish."

Now it was Martina's turn to blush. Sam was just glad to have Evangeline's attention on someone else long enough for him to finish off his burrito. "You have seen, now, what we face," Evangeline went on. "Gideon Arnold will stop at nothing to get his hands on my ancestor's weapon. He has killed for it, and he is more than willing to kill again." For a moment her eyes went back out to the flag, now flapping more strongly in the breeze, and Sam remembered that it was her father who Arnold had killed.

"If Arnold gets what he wants," she went on, "there is no telling what kind of destruction he might cause. So I ask you both—will you continue with us? You've heard what happened during the Civil War—well, we need to do that again. We have Franklin's key, but there are six more artifacts we need to find before we can recover the Founders' weapon. All of them must be taken to safety now that the secret locations have been compromised. And with so many of the other Founders missing or unwilling to help—" Evangeline paused, the worry plain on her face. "I would trust Theodore with my very life, such is my faith in him. But one young man, even with my help, cannot do this alone. I'm afraid you children are our only hope." She took a deep breath and looked at Sam and Martina. "I know it's unfair of me to ask this of you, but I have no choice. So I'll ask again: Will you join us?"

Theo pulled down his sunglasses a little, watching intently as he awaited their answer.

Sam hesitated, thinking back to the face he had seen in the mirror.

So which Sam Solomon was he? The one who hacked into school computers to change his friend's grades, or the one who did his best to save the country from treachery that went back more than two hundred years?

Sam realized, to his surprise, that he already knew. He'd promised his mother that this trip would change him, and it had. He couldn't keep pulling dumb pranks and winning puzzle contests, not when he knew what was really going on.

Besides, even though yesterday had been terrifying and crazy and painful, he had to admit it had been exciting too. It wasn't like he could go back to sneaking into the principal's office, not when he'd survived falling into flooded mine shafts and solving underwater puzzles and escaping from crazy castles built in the middle of deserts. And could he really leave Marty Always-Wright and Theo the Giant to have all the fun without him?

No way.

"Yeah," he said. "I'm in."

"Me too!" Martina's eyes were sparkling. "After all, Sam will just bungle it without me. We can't leave the saving of the world to somebody with ketchup all over his chin."

Sam scrubbed at his chin, glaring at Martina. She stuck her tongue out at him. Theo shook his head, chuckling, and slid his sunglasses back into place.

"Excellent." Evangeline looked pleased. "Now we can move on to the next mission."

"I'm not sure how." Sam leaned against a pillar. "We've got to find the next Founder's vault, I get it. But we don't even know where to look!"

"My ancestor would hardly leave us with no direction, Mr. Solomon," Evangeline said, smiling.

"Yeah, we found his clue, the one in the key, but that Arnold guy took it. Didn't Theo tell you?"

"He didn't take our memories, though." Martina dug a pen out of one of her pockets and flipped her note from Evangeline over, sketching quickly on the back—a mountain, a horned animal, a foot, a person with a flattened head. "This is it, right? Sam, you saw it too. Did I miss anything?"

Sam came to look at the picture with Martina. "You've got it, but what does it mean? It's a mountain. A mountain with a goat. That's a goat, right?"

"Has to be the Rocky Mountains," Martina said. "Mountain goats are native to the Rockies."

"Okay, fine. That's one big mountain chain, though," Sam pointed out. "We can't check out every mountain in the Rockies."

"That's why the Founders left us the other clues."

"Unless they were just doodling. What are these pictures supposed to mean? A black foot? A guy with a flat head?"

"Do they always sound like this?" Evangeline asked Theo.

He nodded. "It's how they work."

"Carry on, then," Evangeline said to Sam and Martina, her eyes bright with amusement.

"Flat foot. Black head," Sam mumbled. "I mean, black foot, flat head. I'm not seeing anything here."

"That's it!" Martina exclaimed.

"What's it?"

"Blackfoot! Flathead!"

"Yeah, but, Marty, saying the same words I was saying like they actually mean something doesn't solve the puzzle."

"Ugh, just wait a second! Evangeline, can I borrow your phone?"

"Hey! Google is cheating!" Sam said.

Martina ignored him, tapping on the phone's screen. "Blackfoot and Flathead are the names of two Native

American tribes, Sam. And their ancestral lands are in . . ." She stopped, then waved the phone in front of his face. "Glacier National Park! In Montana! Look, the mountain goat is actually the official symbol of the park. That must be where the next Founder's vault is hidden!"

"Glaciers. You're kidding me," Sam grumbled. "Out of the frying pan"—he gestured at the desert all around them, heating up rapidly as the sun rose—"and into the freezer?"

"Glacier National Park, huh," Theo said. He looked thoughtful.

"We'll stop for some parkas," Evangeline said, rising from her chair. "And some insulated boots, perhaps. Well, no time to waste!"

"I have to pack!" Martina leaped up too. "Oh . . . I don't actually have all that much to pack. That Arnold guy took all my stuff! Can we stop by an outdoor supply place? And a bookstore? And a cartographer's maybe? When are we leaving?"

"Next year, by the sounds of it," said Sam.

Evangeline pointed to a dot in the sky, growing larger by the second. It wasn't long before a white helicopter was settling down on the resort's lawn, setting the American flag whipping frantically in the wind from its rotating blades.

She smiled at Martina. "Does that answer your question?"

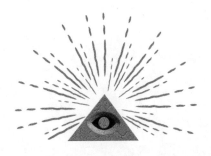

POSTSCRIPT

Dear Mom and Dad,

We're leaving Death Valley today. We hiked in the desert, took
a swim in an underground pool (totally refreshing), and even
got to explore an old abandoned gold mine. I'm learning a ton
of stuff about history. Did you know that Ben Franklin had
a list of thirteen virtues he tried to live by? I'm never going
to forget any of them! This actually is the trip of a lifetime.
When you see me again, I'll be a different person. I hope
you'll be proud of the new . . .

Sam

Sam, Martina, and Theo are back in a new, exhilarating adventure set in Glacier National Park. It will be up to them, and the readers, to solve the puzzles before it's too late.

Don't miss *The Eagle's Quill*!

SECRETS
OF THE SEVEN

The
EAGLE'S QUILL

SARAH L. THOMSON
BLOOMSBURY

To my dear and trusted friend Josiah Hodge, greetings.

My thoughts and hopes will travel westward with you, Captain Lewis, Lieutenant Clark, and the other members of the Corps of Discovery. How I wish I might accompany you, to discover the length and breadth of our land, to encounter tribes unknown to us, and to come face-to-face at last with the distant and mighty Pacific. The trials and difficulties of life here in the President's House seem petty and unimportant compared with the quest that you and your companions are undertaking.

And you, my friend, bear a responsibility that no other member of the expedition can share. With this letter, I entrust the Eagle's Quill to your care. The Quill penned the Declaration that gave our nation its birth; it will now help to protect that nation from enemies within and without. You know that our enemies are many, some even in our own midst.

Keep the Quill safe at all times. When you reach your destination, hide it in a most secret and protected location known only to yourself. Reveal its existence to no one except, as your life nears its end, to one of your own family whom you can trust to carry on the charge. I pray, as do all the Founders, that we will never be called upon to use the secret the Quill protects. But that is for the ages to decide.

Farewell, my friend. In this life, we shall not meet again. But our shared duty to our newborn country will keep our hearts and minds close for as long as our lives last.

With most sincere esteem
and regard,

Thomas Jefferson

Sam took another bite of his Snickers bar and chewed slowly, unable to take his eyes from the view outside the helicopter window.

For the past few hours, he'd been watching the flat, dry, dusty landscape of Nevada sort of crumple and heave itself upward, first into gentle green hills, then into taller slopes. After a stop to refuel, they had finally reached Montana, where towering peaks stabbed up through pine forests into a sky that was so blue it practically glowed.

Sam had never seen mountains this big before. This steep. This . . . this . . . *mountainy.* The sheer size of it all was making his brain reel. He could almost hear a soundtrack playing in the distance: "O beautiful, for spacious skies, for amber waves of grain. For purple mountain majesties . . ."

And to make things even better, nobody was trying to kill him or any of his friends. Right this minute, anyway. Lately Sam had learned not to take that kind of thing for granted.

The person sitting next to Sam poked him with a finger. Sam turned to glance at Martina—Marty—Wright. Her eyes were lit up with excitement behind her glasses, and her black hair, chopped off at the level of her chin in a line so straight you could use it for a ruler, swung beneath her headset. Under a fleece jacket she wore a purple T-shirt that said THE PAST, THE PRESENT, AND THE FUTURE WALKED INTO A BAR. IT WAS TENSE.

"Did you know that Glacier National Park was the tenth national park to be established?" Marty asked. She was speaking into the headset; Sam wore a similar one. The noise from the helicopter rotors was so loud that without the headsets on you couldn't hear a word anybody said.

"Nope," Sam said. He didn't add that he didn't care much either. Marty knew a lot of stuff, and she liked to share it. Sometimes it could be irritating, but there had been times in the past few days when the things Marty knew had saved Sam's life.

Still, that didn't mean he had to listen to her twenty-four/seven, did it?

"And did you know—" she started to say.

"So, listen," he interrupted her. "What do you think we're going to be looking for when we land? Got any ideas about what our old pal Ben Franklin would have wanted us to find in Montana?"

"Do tell us some more about Glacier National Park, Ms. Wright," cut in a cool voice, one that belonged to Evangeline Temple. She was seated across from Marty, and when Sam glanced at her, she skewered him with her gaze and nodded toward the helicopter pilot. Obviously she wanted Sam to stop talking into his headset when the guy could hear.

"Well, it has one of the largest remaining grizzly bear populations in the lower forty-eight states," Marty said with enthusiasm. "Did you know that some scientists consider polar bears to be a subspecies of grizzly bears? And how about this . . ."

Sam scratched behind his left ear, and while his hand was up there, pressed the button that turned his headset from *on* to *off*. Marty's voice went silent, although her mouth kept moving. Sam smiled and nodded, wide-eyed and eager, which seemed to make Marty happy. She kept on moving her mouth as Sam turned his face back to the window.

This time, however, he focused his gaze not on the landscape whizzing past, but on the faint reflection he could see of Evangeline and the person next to her.

Tall and slim, her dark hair streaked with white and very smooth under her headset, Evangeline seemed to be listening to Marty, but it was hard to tell. For all Sam knew, she'd switched off her headset just as he had, and she was busy daydreaming about Betsy Ross singing a karaoke version of "Yankee Doodle" with some steel drums for backup.

Next to her, Theo—Theodore Washington—slouched in a seat that looked too small for him. But everything looked too small for Theo. He made the whole helicopter seem like something from a kid's G.I. Joe collection.

Theo was staring out of the window just as Sam had been, without a word to say. That wasn't unusual. Sam had known Theo only a few days, and the one thing he knew for sure about the big guy was that Theo didn't speak up unless it was to say something that mattered.

As Sam watched, Theo frowned, and his fingers began to tap out a restless rhythm on the armrest of his seat. And for some reason that Sam couldn't quite put his finger on, Theo didn't look like a guy who was staying quiet because he didn't have anything to say. Instead he looked like a guy who had plenty to say but wasn't saying any of it.

Weird. But then everything had been weird for days now, when it hadn't been terrifying, astonishing, or just plain impossible to believe.

And life didn't show signs of getting back to normal anytime soon.

Sam kept watching the two faces, Evangeline's pale ivory and Theo's dark brown, both superimposed on a rushing landscape of conifers and rocky peaks and cloud-swept sky. He really wished he knew a bit more about the things Theo wasn't saying. Evangeline too. The pair of them had not always been exactly up front about what they knew and what they were planning.

In fact, there were times when they had straight-out lied.

Evangeline had pretended to be running a puzzle con-test, the kind of thing Sam loved to enter. The American Dream Contest. Sam had been so excited when he'd got-ten that letter in the silver envelope, the one that said he'd won. His prize? The trip of a lifetime.

Well, Evangeline sure hadn't lied about that part.

What she hadn't told him—not at first, anyway—was that this trip of a lifetime would involve a crazy trek across the entire country, trying to find seven artifacts hidden in seven secret locations. Those artifacts were the key to finding some bizarre super-weapon from way back in Revolutionary War times, something Ben Frank-lin himself had invented. That's what Evangeline claimed, anyway.

Sam dug around in his pockets and fished out a crum-pled receipt and a chewed-up ballpoint pen. He smoothed the receipt on his knee and wrote, *Any idea what kind of weapon Ben F. would dream up? Death ray? Nuclear bomb? Photon torpedo?*

He passed the note to Marty. She looked down at it and frowned, shook her head, snatched the pen from his hand, and wrote until she ran out of receipt.

She handed the note back. *Really, Sam? Nobody in Revolutionary Days even knew what an atom was. How could Ben Franklin come up with—*

Marty found a little notebook in the inside pocket of her jacket. She flipped it open and finished what she had been writing.

—a nuclear weapon?

Sam took the notebook from her and wrote. *So no bomb. What else could it be? Ideas?*

Insufficient data, Marty wrote back. *For now we have to concentrate on finding the next artifact.*

Sam opened Marty's notebook to a new page. Quickly, he drew a sketch of the picture that had sent them to Montana—a mountain, a goat, a black foot, and a guy with a flat head. It had been Marty who had figured out what the images meant; she was nearly as good at puzzles as Sam was. Nearly.

The mountain and the goat together meant the Rockies, and the body parts stood for the Blackfoot and the Flathead, Native American tribes who lived near Glacier National Park. If Marty was right, and if they were very, very lucky, they should be able to find their second artifact somewhere inside that park.

The things had been hidden—way too well, as far as Sam was concerned—by a secret society called the Founders, descendants of the Founding Fathers themselves. There were two of them right here in this helicopter—Evangeline, a descendant of Benjamin Franklin, and Theo, the several-times great-nephew of George Washington.

The Founders had stashed the artifacts, and then they'd filled their hiding places with puzzles and traps, making sure that only the right people would get their hands on stuff like the key that Benjamin Franklin had flown from his famous kite. The key that, yesterday, Sam had actually held in his hand.

And Evangeline and Theo had not mentioned any of this. Not right away, at least. Sure, they'd come clean now—after everything that had happened in Death Valley, where Sam and Marty and Theo had fallen down flooded mine shafts and solved deadly underground puzzles and nearly been electrocuted—Marty *had* actually been electrocuted!—and escaped scary guys with guns.

But did that mean, Sam wondered, that Evangeline and Theo had told him and Marty about everything? Or did those two have more surprises in store?

Sam shook his head, shoved the notebook back at Marty, lifted the last of his Snickers bar to his mouth, and felt his teeth close on paper. He'd eaten the whole thing, barely tasting it. What a waste. He licked a smear of chocolate off the wrapper just as the helicopter tilted, and his stomach squeezed itself up against the back of his throat. The ground outside his window swooped closer. They were coming in for a landing.

Marty put the notebook back in her pocket, and then she reached toward Sam's head and pressed his headset's *on* button. "So, *like I was saying*"—she zapped a pointed look in his direction—"Lewis and Clark wouldn't have gotten anywhere without Sacagawea. And all she gets is one dinky little dollar coin that won't even go in most vending machines. Totally unfair. And—"

"We'll be hitting the ground in Whitefish in about ten minutes or so," crackled the pilot's voice, cutting off Marty midsentence. He'd probably figured out that waiting for Marty to be done talking was like waiting for the sun to be done shining. It would happen eventually, but could you really hold out for several billion years?

Sam listened to Marty's fifty most fascinating facts about the Lewis and Clark Expedition while the helicopter got lower and lower, finally touching down on a landing strip. Sam was the first one out the door.

It wasn't much of an airport, he thought as he jumped down to the tarmac. A couple of little planes and choppers like theirs were scattered here and there, and one low building was in the distance. He drew in a deep breath of the fresh, cool air and shivered a little. Quite a difference from the blazing heat of Death Valley, where he had woken up this morning.

But it wasn't just the chill in the breeze that made that little hint of uneasiness creep up Sam's spine. One of the many things that Evangeline and Theo had failed to mention early on was that the four of them weren't the only ones trying to get their hands on the Founders' artifacts. They had competition in this race. The other team was headed up by a scary guy named Flintlock, who worked for a man called Gideon Arnold.

Sam remembered Arnold's pale, almost colorless eyes, and the icy way they had looked at Sam and his friends over the barrel of a gun. The guy knew how to hold a grudge, that was for sure. He was still furious about what had happened to his who-knew-how-many-times-great-grandfather, Benedict Arnold himself. America's most infamous traitor. And, more important, Gideon Arnold was ready to kill anybody who got between him and the Founders' artifacts.

Could Arnold be here right now? Watching them? Sam brooded about that while the four of them hauled their suitcases through the airport and Evangeline waved a hand at a taxi waiting by the curb. Could some of Arnold's spies be hanging around in baggage claim? Could the taxi driver be in Arnold's pay? It wasn't impossible. One thing Sam had learned on his little jaunt through Death Valley was not to ever, under any circumstances, underestimate Gideon Arnold.

The taxi swept them along a highway and into the little town of Whitefish. They rolled over a bridge with a shallow river flowing underneath and piled out of the cab when their driver announced that they had made it downtown.

It didn't look like much of a downtown to Sam. No skyscrapers, maybe two traffic lights, about a dozen wooden storefronts lining either side of the street. One sign declared that its building was the WILD, WILDER, WILDEST WEST SALOON!!! With three exclamation marks. Sam counted them. Next door was a store with a wide window full of ten-gallon hats and intricately tooled cowboy boots.

Evangeline paid the cabbie (who didn't seem to be an agent of Gideon Arnold's after all) and asked him where they could find a good outdoor supply store. "We will need to do some shopping," she said as the driver took off. She pointed up the street. Marty headed in that direction, in front of Sam. Evangeline and Theo trailed behind.

"Just look at those mountains," Marty gushed, pointing to the view at the end of the street. She tipped her face up to appreciate the snow-covered slabs of rock, glowing in the amber light of early afternoon. "Quite a change from the desert, right, Sam? Sam?"

"Uh-huh," Sam grunted. Marty was staring around like a tourist, and Evangeline and Theo were muttering together, so it looked like it was up to Sam to keep an eye out for the bad guys. Trouble was, he didn't know exactly what he was looking for. It wasn't like Arnold's employees wore little name tags announcing, "Hi! My name is Bob, and I work for a homicidal maniac!"

Anyway, every other person in this little town seemed somehow out of place to Sam's eyes. It was because most of the people walking by were tourists, he realized. They wore hiking boots and fleece jackets and multipocketed fishermen's vests, and they were consulting maps or guidebooks or looking around like Marty, marveling at the scenery.

Sam followed Marty down the sidewalk, passing a drugstore, a gallery full of Native American artifacts, places advertising helicopter tours and white-water rafting, and a bakery selling cinnamon buns that smelled so good Sam nearly forgot he was supposed to be watching out for sinister henchmen.

"We have to—" Sam heard Theo say from behind him, but he didn't finish the sentence.

"We have to *go where the clues take us*," Evangeline answered, her low voice full of meaning. "No matter how hard it is."

Bang!

© Mark Mattos

SARAH L. THOMSON is an award-winning author who has published more than thirty books for young readers, including the Secrets of the Seven series, *Deadly Flowers*, and *Dragon's Egg*. Sarah lives in Portland, Maine, with her daughter and her two cats. Her daughter helps with inspiration, and her cats help by lying on the piece of paper she needs most.

www.sarahlthomson.com
www.secretsoftheseven.com